The low growl sent chills up her spine.

"What is it, boy?" Julianne pulled her gun from the holster on her waist and glanced around the parking lot as if searching for whatever had gotten her dog's attention.

"Does he do this often?" Brody put a hand on his gun, too.

"Only when he senses danger."

They'd taken a few steps toward her vehicle when Thunder abuptly stopped and backed up a step. He growled low in his throat, and pushed at Julianne with his nose, as if to move her out of the way.

"What is it?" The moment Julianne said the words, Brody saw a figure running away from the parking lot.

He grabbed her arm. "We have to get out of here. Now!"

CLASSIFIED K-9 UNIT:
These lawmen solve the toughest cases
with the help of their brave canine partners

Laura Scott is a nurse by day and an author by night. She has always loved romance and read faith-based books by Grace Livingston Hill in her teenage years. She's thrilled to have published over twelve books for Love Inspired Suspense. She has two adult children and lives in Milwaukee, Wisconsin, with her husband of thirty years. Please visit Laura at laurascottbooks.com, as she loves to hear from her readers.

Books by Laura Scott

Love Inspired Suspense

Classified K-9 Unit

Sheriff

Callahan Confidential

Shielding His Christmas Witness
The Only Witness

SWAT: Top Cops

Wrongly Accused
Down to the Wire
Under the Lawman's Protection
Forgotten Memories
Holiday on the Run
Mirror Image

Visit the Author Profile page at Harlequin.com for more titles.

SHERIFF

LAURA SCOTT

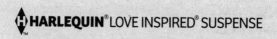

HARLEQUIN® LOVE INSPIRED® SUSPENSE

Special thanks and acknowledgment to Laura Scott for her participation in the Classified K-9 Unit miniseries.

Recycling programs for this product may not exist in your area.

LOVE INSPIRED BOOKS

ISBN-13: 978-0-373-45704-5

Sheriff

Copyright © 2017 by Harlequin Books S.A.

www.Harlequin.com

Printed in U.S.A.

Answer me when I call to You, my righteous God.
Give me relief from my distress;
have mercy on me and hear my prayer.
—*Psalms* 4:1

This book is dedicated to a dear friend
and wonderful fan, Vicki Lynn Christman,
and her adorable Westie Sophie. Here's the K-9 story
you've been waiting for! Thanks for being
such a strong supporter of my books.

ONE

The low rumble of a car engine caused FBI Agent Julianne Martinez to freeze in her tracks. She quickly gave her K-9 partner, Thunder, the hand signal for stay. The Big Thicket region of east Texas was densely covered with trees and brush. This particular area of the woods had also been oddly silent.

Until now.

Envisioning the map in her pocket that Dylan O'Leary, the team's technical guru, had drawn up for them, she realized she must have gone too far south, heading toward the rural road, barely paved, instead of north to the cabin where their missing colleague, FBI Agent Jake Morrow, could very well be held captive by the criminal mobster Angus Dupree.

Moving silently, she angled toward the road, sucking in a harsh breath when she caught a glimpse of a white-and-black prison van.

What in the world? The van abruptly halted with enough force that it rocked back and forth. Frowning, she edged closer to get a better look.

The reason the van had stopped was that there was a black SUV sitting diagonally across the road, barricading the way.

Reacting instinctively to the perceived threat, Julianne rushed forward. As she drew her revolver, she heard a bang and a crash followed by a man tumbling out of the back of the prison van. The large bald guy dressed in prison orange made a beeline toward the SUV. Another man stood in the center of the road pointing a weapon at the van driver, who held his hands up in the air in a gesture of surrender.

A prison break!

"Stop!" Julianne pointed her weapon and shot at the gunman, hoping, praying she could save the van driver's life. Her aim was true, and the assailant flinched, staggering backward, but didn't go down. Instead he turned toward her, a fierce expression etched on his face.

He had to be wearing body armor.

Seconds later, the situation spiraled out of control. The gunman shot the driver through the windshield, then came running directly at Julianne. She gave her K-9 partner two hand-signal commands.

Hide. Stay.

Good boy, she thought, as Thunder slinked behind a large tree. He was an English foxhound, and his brown-and-black coat, along with his black FBI bulletproof vest, worked well as camouflage. She didn't want him to get hurt, but she also needed him to protect her back.

Just as she'd protect his.

She ducked behind a tree, then took a steadying breath. Tightening her grip on her 9 mm, she peered around to where she'd last seen the shooter. She fired at him once again, then ducked behind the tree.

Keep moving.

Julianne eased from one tree to the next as Thunder watched, waiting for her signal. Now the silence was suffocating, the slightest rustle of a leaf unbearably loud.

When she couldn't take the quiet for another moment,

she peeked out trying to identify where the gunman was located.

Crack!

She ducked, feeling the whiz of the bullet miss her by a fraction of an inch, a piece of bark flying off the tree. The perp was roughly twenty feet in front of her, far closer than she'd anticipated.

After a long moment, she was about to risk another glance, when the assailant popped out from behind a tree. He looked her square in the eye, the barrel of his gun pointing directly at her chest.

"Stop right there," he shouted in a hoarse voice. "Put your hands in the air."

Angry that she hadn't anticipated the gunman's move, Julianne held his gaze, refusing to glance at Thunder, hoping the thug hadn't seen her partner.

"Put your hands in the air!" he repeated harshly.

She continued to stare at him, knowing if she did as the gunman demanded, he'd shoot where she stood. He'd already killed the van driver, what more did he have to lose?

Nothing.

So why hadn't he shot her already? Was he looking for information?

"Fire that gun, and I'll plant a bullet between your eyes," a familiar, deep husky Texan drawl came from out of nowhere.

Brody Kenner?

The gunman jerked and glanced to his left. In that split second she fired at the arm holding his gun. Her FBI training didn't fail her. He screamed in pain. Blood spurted from his right arm, and he dropped the weapon.

Then he turned and fled.

"Thunder, fetch!" Julianne didn't bother to look over

at the man she'd once loved, the man who'd just saved her life, but remained focused on not losing the perp.

She wasn't nearly as fast as Thunder when it came to running through the woods, dodging trees. And it seemed like just mere moments later when she heard tires squealing as a car drove away. She slowed down, gasping for breath, knowing it was too late.

The gunman and whoever had run from the prison van had escaped.

Frustration clawing through her, she headed over to the vehicle to check on the driver. The poor man was dead. She murmured a prayer, wishing she had something to cover him with before turning her attention to the issue at hand.

"Thunder?"

Hearing nothing but silence, her heart lodged in her throat. Had the dog jumped into the getaway car? Or had someone attacked him? But then her partner came bounding back through the woods toward her. When he saw her he let out his usual, strangely musical foxhound howl.

"Good boy," she said, bending over to give him a good rub, scratching the soft spot between his ears. "Good boy, Thunder."

"What in the world was that noise?"

Taking a deep breath, she straightened and turned to face Brody Kenner. He was taller and broader than she remembered, but had the same dark hair and brilliant blue eyes that she'd tried not to dream about after he'd broken her heart six years ago. He was dressed in a deep brown uniform with a sheriff's star on his chest.

So he was the Clover County sheriff now?

Somehow she wasn't surprised.

Brody looked good. Better than good. Her chest felt tight and she had to concentrate in order to breathe normally.

What was wrong with her? What she and Brody once had was over and done with. Had been for a long time. A familiar flash of resentment twisted, turned into something softer. Regret? Seeing him again, she hated to admit that maybe things weren't as finished as she'd wanted them to be. Just looking at him standing there, so big and strong and formidable, wreaked havoc with her emotions.

Erupting her buried feelings to the surface where they had the power to hurt her all over again.

Brody's pulse still pounded at how Julianne had nearly been shot to death right in front of his eyes.

What was she doing here? As far as he knew, she hadn't stepped foot in the Lone Star State since joining the FBI academy six years ago.

"Thanks for helping." Julianne's clipped voice was colder than the Clover River in January.

"Hey, what are friends for?" He grinned, but she didn't smile back. Her long ebony hair was pulled back from her face and her large dark eyes, a legacy from her Puerto Rican father, never made it easy to guess what she was thinking.

She wore khaki slacks paired with a dark shirt, a small FBI K-9 logo over the left breast pocket. He'd known Julianne had left Texas to attend the academy but hadn't known the FBI had a K-9 unit. Or that she'd joined it. Although she always had loved dogs.

She frowned. "How did you get here so fast?"

He lifted a brow. As the sheriff he was the one who should be questioning her about what she was doing trampling through the woods in his county. "I was following the prison van." Then he scowled at where the van sat stationary in the road, the dead driver slumped over the steering wheel. "Obviously not closely enough."

If Julianne thought his actions strange, she didn't say anything. This wasn't the time to bring up how he'd intended to watch his former best friend, Nathan Otwell, walk into the maximum security prison for himself. It had taken Brody a long time to gather the evidence he needed to prove his former juvie roommate had actually participated in luring troubled young men and women into drug running, prostitution and human slavery.

Several months of fourteen-hour days, because he hadn't wanted to believe it.

Until he'd seen the evidence with his own eyes.

"I'm sorry the prisoner got away." She swiped a hand across her forehead. "He must have had a backup plan."

He nodded, glancing curiously at her dog, sitting straight up at her side. When faced with a stranger, he didn't bark, aside of the weird howl he'd let out.

What had she called him? Thunder?

"Excuse me, I need to call this in." She slid her service weapon into her hip holster and then pulled a mobile phone from her pants pocket.

"Wait a minute. Are you here in Clover on official business?" Brody scowled. The feds were supposed to notify local law enforcement when they were doing an investigation.

As a courtesy at the very least.

But he hadn't been told anything at all about an FBI investigation taking place in his county. Which was why he'd been shocked to find Julianne facing the wrong side of a gun.

"Yes." She didn't elaborate, which only added fuel to the slow burn of anger and resentment in his belly.

What, had he *really* thought she'd come back to find him after six years?

No, of course not. He'd given up on that foolish hope

a long time ago. She'd made her decision, one that hadn't included him.

"Max? It's Julianne. I have a situation." A brief pause as she listened, then nodded. "Okay."

Brody ground his teeth, wondering who Max was. Her partner? Or a personal friend? Something more than a friend?

He cocked his head, listening to the sound of someone making their way through the woods.

A tall, muscular man with short blond hair emerged from the brush, a caramel-brown female boxer at his side. The man's rugged face bore a concerned look. "Julianne? What happened? Are you all right?"

"I'm fine." There was a sharp edge to her tone. "I would have gotten the assailant if he hadn't been wearing body armor."

"Who are you?" the man, who he guessed was Max, demanded, noticing Brody.

"Clover County Sheriff Brody Kenner." Brody folded his arms across his chest. "Who are y'all? And what brings the FBI to my neck of the woods?"

He didn't appreciate the silent exchange Julianne shared with Max.

"FBI Special Agent in Charge, Max West." The fed stepped closer and offered his hand. "My partner, Opal, and this is Agent Julianne Martinez and her partner, Thunder."

Brody shook Max's hand, more pleased than he had a right to be to know his former flame wasn't married. "I know Julianne, we went to college together."

"I see." Max glanced at Julianne who still wasn't smiling.

"A guy I sent to prison just escaped," Brody continued.

"His associate came after Agent Martinez. He took a shot at her, but thankfully missed, although not by much."

"Are you sure you're all right?" Max asked, reaching out to put a hand on Julianne's arm.

She shook off his grip. "I'm fine, but Brody is right. I witnessed the prison break. The perp who shot at me killed the van driver. I managed to hit him in the arm so all the hospitals in a hundred-mile radius need to be put on alert."

"I'll take care of it," Brody assured her. Using his radio, he notified his dispatcher to put all the deputies on notice. He also ordered roadblocks on every major highway and for his deputies to follow up with the law enforcement agencies and hospitals located nearby. From the way the gunman had been bleeding, he felt sure the guy wouldn't last too long without medical care. Lastly, he requested several of his deputies to report to this location in order to attend to the crime scene.

When he finished he overheard Julianne and Max speaking in low tones.

"Y'all still haven't told me what you're doing here." Brody stepped up, making it clear he wasn't going to be ignored.

"Following up a lead," Max said, resting his hand on his boxer's head.

Brody bit back a flash of impatience. Why the secrecy? "What kind of lead? Who are you looking for?"

Once again, Julianne and Max exchanged a long look, as if debating how much to tell him.

He scowled, crossed his arms over his chest and waited.

"The information I'm about to tell you is classified, understand?" Max said. Brody nodded his agreement, so he continued, "We're part of the FBI Tactical K-9 Unit, working a case related to one of our agents, Jake Morrow, who went missing several weeks ago."

"Missing?" He frowned. How often did FBI agents, especially those in some sort of secret elite team, go missing? "That's strange."

"I don't disagree. We're here because we received an anonymous tip via a disposable cell phone, one that we were unable to trace, that Jake is being held in a secluded cabin in the area," Julianne explained. "We're not sure who our informant is, but we're determined to check out each clue no matter how improbable, so if you don't mind, we need to get back to work."

"I'm afraid I do mind," Brody drawled.

She ignored him, looking at her superior. "What did you find at your cabin?"

"Opal didn't alert on anything. It's deserted and looks as if it's been that way for a long time."

"Okay, then that leaves the cabin here as the primary search zone." Julianne pulled some sort of computer-engineered map out of her pocket.

"What's that?" Brody asked, stepping closer to get a better look.

"A map put together by Dylan O'Leary, our team's technical expert. He's located back at headquarters, helping to coordinate our activities. Here." She tapped the map, glancing up at Max. "This is where I veered off track. We need to head due north."

"Maybe you didn't understand what I meant," Brody interjected. "I'm going with you."

She frowned. "Thanks, but that's not necessary. We can take it from here."

"This may be your jurisdiction, Agent Martinez." He emphasized her formal title with a hint of sarcasm. "But this is my county, and I'm going with you. Whether y'all like it or not."

She stared at him for several long moments. "What about the crime scene here?"

"My deputies will be here any moment—they'll take care of things."

He wasn't going to let anything change his mind. Whatever Julianne and Max were doing was just as important as searching for Nate Otwell.

Now that Julianne had reappeared in his life, there was no way she was going anywhere without him.

"I see you're just as stubborn as ever, Brody." There was no time to waste, so Julianne didn't bother trying to talk him out of joining them.

She hadn't been able to convince him to believe in her, to come with her to join the FBI academy six years ago, either. The man could teach stubborn to an ox.

"Are you sure you want to keep going?" Max asked for the third time. "I can take over."

"Yes, I'm sure. Stop asking already." She was annoyed at the way her boss was treating her, as if she were some helpless damsel in distress who couldn't hold her own.

She was a trained FBI agent. Getting shot at came with the territory.

And if she were honest, she'd admit that seeing Brody again, hearing her name spoken in his familiar southern drawl, had shaken her up more than any gunman. Especially since it looked as if her ex wouldn't be leaving anytime soon.

Ignoring the four deputies who'd just arrived at the crime scene, she retraced her steps, looking for the evidence bag she'd dropped in her mad rush to stop the prison break. Fifty yards back, she found the sack containing an old shirt belonging to Jake Morrow. Kneeling on the ground, she opened the bag and encouraged Thunder to take a deep sniff.

Thunder buried his nose in the bag for several long seconds.

"Find, Thunder." She pointed north in the direction where the cabin was located. "Find Jake."

Thunder's tail wagged, then his nose went to the ground. He walked in a few circles, then trotted north. Julianne followed, trying to ignore Brody dogging her heels.

As they made their way through the woods, the brush grew more and more dense. Twice Thunder made a few circles, as if he'd caught a whiff of something important, but he never alerted.

The trees offered significant shade from the hot May sun, but that didn't mean it was cool. Sweat beaded along Julianne's scalp, rolling down her temples.

"Do you know the people responsible for Agent Morrow's disappearance?" Brody asked.

Julianne glanced at him. If in fact Angus Dupree had a cabin in the area, Brody deserved to know. "We have reason to believe that Jake was captured by a highly organized crime family headed up by Reginald Dupree. We raided a warehouse owned by the Duprees, capturing the head of the family, Reginald, but his second-in-command, Angus, got away. Angus is running the show now. Upon further investigation we found evidence that Jake had been there. Unfortunately he's been missing ever since."

"How long ago?"

"Too long." Julianne's voice was curt. "But I'm convinced that with Thunder's help, we'll find him."

"Are you sure your dog knows where he's going?" Brody asked as they wedged their way through a particularly dense thicket. "I can't believe there's a cabin anywhere in this mess."

"He knows," she said in a terse tone. "Besides, I have a map."

"I'd like to see it."

Julianne shook her head, there wasn't time, besides, they'd already told Brody more information than they should considering the confidential nature of their team. Keeping her gaze trained on Thunder, she noticed her partner was slowing down thanks to the denseness of the woods and she wondered how much farther they'd be able to go. By her estimation, the cabin was still a good mile away.

A mile that may as well be twenty based on the difficult terrain.

"I should have brought a machete," she grumbled as she forced her way through another bush.

"Wouldn't help." Brody was so close she was surrounded by the spicy scent of his aftershave intermixed with his unique male essence. Breathing through her mouth to avoid his intoxicating scent, she tried her best to fight the memories.

Both the good and the bad.

Don't, she warned herself. *Don't go there.*

Abruptly, Thunder veered right, heading straight for a large tree. Julianne held her breath, closely watching her partner.

Thunder sniffed along the base of the tree, then jerked his head back to the right side of the tree. Then he scratched at the spot and plopped down on his butt, staring at the ground as if there was something to see.

"What in the world?" Brody sounded incredulous.

Julianne glanced at Brody. Max and Opal were bringing up the rear. Opal was a bomb-sniffing dog, so Max had given Julianne and Thunder the lead in attempting to pick up the trail.

"Thunder alerted on Jake's scent. He was here, Max. Jake Morrow was here."

"I see that, but where's the cabin?" her captain asked.

Good question. She joined Thunder. "Good boy," she praised him. "Good boy. You found Jake."

She stood near the large tree for several moments, then pulled Dylan's map out again.

"Max? Hand me your binoculars."

Brody took them from Max and brought them over. Raising them to her eyes, she peered through the magnified lenses and incrementally moved the glasses from right to left.

There! She used the dial to sharpen the image.

"I found it," she said excitedly. "There's a house, not a cabin, but a large house roughly three hundred yards away. The only problem is, I don't see a driveway or even a path that could be used to get in there. All I see are trees."

"There has to be a way in," Max insisted.

She inched the binoculars over the wooded area, then stopped abruptly when she saw the wire. "There's a chain-link fence well disguised with brush and trees, topped by barbed wire." She pulled the glasses from her eyes and turned to her boss. "This has to be it, Max. It reeks of Dupree."

"Yeah, but how are we going to get in? Obviously not on foot," he said.

Max was right. She battled a wave of frustration. They were so close. She knew Jake Morrow was being held against his will somewhere inside that house.

They just needed to figure out how to get in to rescue him.

TWO

"**I** know a way," Brody drawled, drawing skeptical looks by the FBI agents. The way the dog had alerted on the trail had been impressive, but he didn't appreciate the way the feds acted as if he wasn't even there.

Especially Julianne. Her indifference hurt, more than it should have.

They'd retreated from the woods, returning to the road. Two of his deputies' vehicles were parked on either side of the prison van, and Brody knew that he needed to head over there to talk to them. But not yet.

She stared at him. "How?"

"From the air." He waved a hand. "I'm a trained para-trooper, I can parachute down landing inside the compound."

Genuine surprise widened her eyes. "Brilliant." She swung toward Max, who nodded in agreement.

"We need to contact Dylan, see if we can get a chopper here, ASAP," Max said. "Not too close, though, because we don't want anyone from inside the compound to hear it."

Brody scowled. "Para-jumping with dogs can be dangerous."

"We learned to do this in our training program," Julianne said in a brisk tone. "We can go in alone, no reason for you to come along."

"Yes, there is. My county, my problem." He couldn't stand the thought of her going in without him and possibly facing an ambush. "Besides, this will be tricky. It might be better if you stay here in the woods as backup in case the whole thing goes south."

She took a step closer and jabbed her finger into his sternum. "Listen, Brody, this is *our* case and I'm going in. You want to come along? Fine. I'm not staying behind. Understand?"

The steely determination in her eyes proved he was fighting a lost cause. Julianne had always been driven to prove herself capable and he knew she'd go in no matter what. He wanted to capture her hand and press it against his chest, but he didn't.

She'd only pull away from him, the way she had six years ago.

"Okay, okay. We'll do this, together."

"Max and Opal are going in, too." She tilted her head. "Where did you train to be a paratrooper?"

"Brief stint in the army." Brody didn't want to mention his messed-up knee that had sent him home early. Three surgeries and it was almost as good as new.

Almost.

Unfortunately, the army didn't want to take a chance with his bum knee, so they'd given him a choice, climb the officer ladder or an early honorary discharge. Climbing up the ranks hadn't interested him so he'd returned home and was offered a job as a deputy. Then somehow managed to become elected sheriff the following year.

Hometown hero and all that. Which was ridiculous since he was anything but. Julianne had left him after their disagreement over her best friend Lilly's disappearance.

She'd insisted Lilly would never have run away, despite all the signs that pointed toward the girl doing just that.

Forcing himself to let go of the past, he swept his gaze over the area. "It would be nice to have deputies guard the perimeter, but that means taking them off roadblock duty, something I'm not willing to do." Brody knew even if he could mobilize every officer he had on staff, it still wouldn't be enough.

Max finished his phone call. "Dylan's looking for a place for a chopper to land. He's also looking for an area for us to use as a landing spot near the house. He figures that there must be something to use if the Duprees are using the air to get access."

Despite his annoyance with his authority being usurped, Brody was impressed. "Wish we had those kinds of resources."

"We're getting the chopper, a pilot and one additional staff member." Max's gaze was on Julianne and Brody couldn't help wondering if there was more between the two of them than professionalism. The flash of jealousy was annoying and unwarranted. Julianne's personal life wasn't his business.

No matter how much he wished otherwise.

"Who?" Julianne asked with a frown.

"Zeke Morrow, and his K-9 partner…an Australian shepherd named Cheetah. Zeke asked to join the team weeks ago, and I've been working on getting him assigned as Jake's replacement. The paperwork has finally cleared, and Zeke really wants in on this."

She stared at Max in apparent surprise, but then blew out a breath and nodded. "I get it, Jake's his half brother. If I were in Zeke's place, I'd want in on the mission to find him, too."

"Boss?"

Brody turned to where two of his deputies waited beside the prison van. The other two deputies were combing the area, looking for clues. "Coming. Julianne, I'll need your help with recreating what happened."

She hesitated, but Max nodded. "Go ahead. It will take some time to get things rolling here."

"The sooner we get inside, the better," she muttered. But she fell in step beside Brody and headed over to the van.

Brody did a quick round of introductions. "Deputy Dan Hanson and Deputy Rick Meyer, this is FBI Agent Julianne Martinez."

Julianne offered her hand. "Nice to meet both of you. I'm the one who stumbled across the prison break."

And almost died for her efforts, Brody thought grimly.

Julianne took them through the events step by step. When she got to the part about the gunman telling her to stop and raise her hands in the air, Deputy Rick Meyer interrupted.

"You get a good look at him?"

Julianne nodded. "Yes. About five-ten, weighing roughly 180 but some of that bulk could have been from the body armor. Thin blond greasy hair and narrow, light eyes. He wore a scruffy beard and had a half-inch scar at the bottom left corner of his mouth."

Once again, Brody couldn't help being impressed. "You got a better look at him than I did."

"Really? You're the one who threatened to plant a bullet between his eyes."

"I know, but that was mostly a way to distract him, so that he'd focus on me, instead of you. To be honest, I didn't have a clear shot from where I was standing."

"I managed to hit him in the right arm," Julianne continued. "He dropped his weapon, then took off."

Brody glanced at Thunder. "Your dog might be able to track him for us."

"Yes, but only if you have some clothing of his to provide Thunder the scent to follow. Blood alone won't work."

Brody considered that idea for a moment. He didn't have anything belonging to the gunman, but he certainly had personal items belonging to Nate Otwell, the man who'd escaped.

His former best friend whom Julianne had never completely trusted.

He let out a disgruntled sigh. As much as he didn't want to admit it, there was no way to deny he needed her help, and the dog's, too.

The time had come to fill Julianne in on what had transpired before the prison break.

Even if that meant proving that she may have been right to leave him, six years ago.

Thunder found the gun and they also discovered several drops of blood left behind by the gunman, but of course the trail disappeared at the edge of the road.

"Did you see what kind of vehicle was waiting for him?" Rick asked. Deputy Dan Hanson was sending antagonistic vibes, but Rick Meyer seemed genuinely willing to partner with her.

Maybe Hanson was one of those who resented having women in law enforcement. It wouldn't be the first time she'd had to deal with overblown macho egos. Or the last.

In her line of work, she was often surrounded by an overabundance of testosterone.

"No. I was still making my way through the trees when I heard the vehicle take off."

"Too bad Thunder can't tell us." Brody patted the animal's head and she bit back the urge to snap at him. Thunder wasn't a pet, he was her partner.

"Thunder, heel."

Instantly, the dog came to her side and sat straight upright, waiting for the next command.

"He's on duty, just like I am," she explained when the three men stared in surprise. "We need to figure out our next steps."

"The medical examiner is on his way to pick up the driver's body," Rick said. "We already know the slug should match the weapon you recovered in the woods."

"Keep looking for the other slug," Brody said. "Julianne can show you where she was when the guy fired at her."

"This way." She led the team of deputies to the area where she'd been. "Here's the rent in the tree bark from the path to the bullet."

They'd found the empty shell casing near where the gunman had dropped the weapon, so Julianne held it out for Thunder. "Find, Thunder. Find!"

Her partner went to work, scouring the area and tracking the scent of gunpowder. The ground was covered in leaves, twigs and other brush, but she knew Thunder could find the missing bullet fragment.

Fifteen minutes later, he alerted on the spot, circling the area, scratching at the ground, then dropping onto his rump. Julianne walked over, gently edged the debris aside, and smiled with grim satisfaction.

"Found it."

"Well, I'll be," Rick said in amazement. "That dog is smarter than most of the people I know."

"Good boy." Julianne rubbed his silky ears and slipped him a treat. "Good boy, Thunder."

Dan made a rude noise under his breath, but drew on

gloves then picked up the bullet fragment and dropped it in a specimen bag. "How many shots did he take at you?"

Julianne lifted a brow. "Just the one."

"Hmm." Deputy Hanson took the evidence back to his squad car.

She decided not to waste time worrying about Hanson's opinion of her abilities. Glancing at her watch, she realized roughly ninety minutes had gone by, and she was feeling dehydrated and hungry. Which meant Thunder needed to eat and drink, too. The hour was close to dinnertime and she hadn't had anything to eat since breakfast.

"Max? What's the ETA on the chopper?"

"Two hours, maybe less. They're coming in from Houston and Dylan has found a small airstrip not far from here for them to use. He sent us a secure email with the location. He's still working on an aerial view of the compound."

She wondered how Dylan was holding up back at headquarters while his fiancée, Zara, was training at Quantico to become a part of their team. "We need to take care of the animals. How about I meet you at the chopper in ninety minutes?"

"Sounds good." Max turned and walked with Opal through the woods. No doubt he'd left his vehicle near the cabin he'd investigated before the gunfire rang out.

Julianne headed in the opposite direction, but then halted when Brody came along. "I've got things to do before the jump."

"I know, but we also need to talk about the prison break. I thought we could grab a bite to eat at Rusty's...they have outside tables now, which would work out well for Thunder."

Rusty's was their old hangout, and the last place she wanted to go was tripping down memory lane. But Thunder needed to eat and so did she, so she pushed the past back where it belonged and nodded stiffly.

"Fine, I'll meet you there."

Brody hesitated. She could tell he wanted them to drive together, but too bad, he'd have to get over it.

She needed some time alone before facing him again. Being home for the first time in six years was bad enough, but seeing Brody again?

That was something else entirely.

Brody tried to look at Rusty's through Julianne's eyes, noticing the changes that had been made to the bar/restaurant over the past few years.

The place had been painted a deep forest green with white trim. The tables outside were covered by green-and-white umbrellas to shade customers from the relentless sun. Patrons actually came here for the food, which hadn't been the case when they were young.

Rusty's had blossomed under new management, and he thought for sure Julianne would notice and approve of the changes.

She was late, and he wondered if she'd stood him up. Not her style, but then again, things hadn't ended well between them.

He saw her drive up in a black SUV with a very small K-9 logo on the back. She slid out from behind the wheel followed by Thunder who jumped gracefully to the ground. The years they'd spent apart disappeared as if they'd never happened. She was still as stunning as ever. And he found himself wishing things had turned out differently for them.

After opening the back, she set one dog dish on the ground and filled it with water. After he drank his fill, she fed him from her hand, which he found curious. Only

when the dog was cared for did she cross over to where
he was waiting.

"The outside is different but has the menu changed?"

"Yeah. Joe Clancy runs the place now with his wife, Sue
Ellen." He pushed a menu over. "We'll talk after we order."

A server came over with water and sweet tea, took their
requests then disappeared back inside.

Julianne drew designs in the condensation that collected
on the side of her glass. "It's been a long time since I've
had Texas sweet tea."

Six years, two weeks and three days, but who was
counting?

She finished her water first, then tried the tea. "It's
sweeter than I remember."

"You don't have tea where you live now?"

"I got out of the habit of drinking it." She pushed her
glass aside, sidestepping his not-so-subtle question. "So
tell me. What's the story behind the prison break?"

He held her gaze. "I arrested Nathan Otwell for drug
running, human trafficking and prostitution. The judge
agreed to hold him without bail because of the overwhelming evidence against him."

"Evidence? Like what?"

"I tracked him to an abandoned cabin where he was
holding five people hostage, getting ready to sell them to
the highest bidder." To this day, Brody would never forget
the scene he'd stumbled upon. "Because of my testimony,
Otwell was being transported from our small jail here to
the maximum security prison over in Cadworth County."

"Nathan Otwell," Julianne repeated, her expression incredulous. "I don't know what to say. The guy who escaped was huge and bald, I didn't recognize him as Nate.
I can't believe it."

"Sure you can," Brody countered in an even tone. "You

never liked him in the first place, even before Lilly ran away. You were convinced Lilly's disappearance was the result of foul play just because she and Nate were seeing each other." He paused, then shrugged. "You were right about Nate, though. In the time I was gone in the army, he reverted back to his criminal ways."

She surprised him by reaching over to put her hand on his forearm. "I'm sorry, Brody. I know how much you believed in him. That must have been difficult for you."

For a moment he wished they could go back six years, to the time before their last argument had torn them irrevocably apart. But he knew better than most there was no going back.

He needed to keep moving forward. No matter how difficult.

"It was worse for the people he abused and sold into slavery." He didn't try to hide the bitterness in his tone. "They're the real victims here. And I can't imagine what they're going to think now that he's escaped."

"I know." Her gaze was sympathetic.

"I'm not going to let him get away with it. I need to find Nate, Julianne. I need your help." He gazed down at the dog lying beneath the table at her feet. "Yours and Thunder's."

The dog perked up when he heard his name, his tail thumping on the ground as if in acknowledgment.

"I have to get Max's approval," she warned. "But since I'm an eyewitness to the shooting of the van driver, I'm sure he'll agree. From what you're telling me, we need to get Nate and his accomplice back into custody as soon as possible."

"Thanks."

"Don't thank me, yet. First we need to get into the Dupree compound and hopefully rescue our missing FBI agent. Once we've done that, we'll focus on picking up

Nate's trail. Hopefully he won't have gotten too far, especially with the roadblocks and other measures you've put into place."

"Agreed." He paused, as the server brought their food. They ate in silence for several minutes, enjoying their Tex-Mex meal when Thunder unexpectedly shot to his feet.

"What is it, boy?" Julianne pulled her gun from the holster on her waist and glanced around the parking lot as if searching for whatever had gotten the dog's attention.

"Does he do this often?" Brody put a hand on his firearm, too, but didn't see anything out of place.

For all they knew, Thunder had scented a squirrel. Or some other animal.

But even as the thought filtered through his mind, he rejected the idea. He might not know much about K-9 officers, but he knew they were trained not to be distracted from their duty. And Thunder's duty included protecting Julianne.

"Sometimes, but I don't see anything amiss, do you?"

"No." Brody couldn't deny that having the dog standing on all fours, ready to attack, was unnerving. "Maybe we should take the food to go."

"Works for me." Julianne finally glanced over at him. "We'll be early, but that's okay."

He waved to get the server's attention and pulled out his wallet to pay for the meal. The outside patio was mostly deserted, patrons favoring the air-conditioned inside rather than the hot and humid outside tables.

A low growl rumbled from Thunder's throat.

"He senses danger," Julianne said in a low tone.

Brody nodded and tossed cash on the table. "Forget the leftovers, let's get out of here."

She nodded and fell into step beside him. They'd taken a few steps toward her black SUV when Thunder abruptly stopped and backed up a step. He growled low in his throat and pushed at Julianne with his nose, as if to move her out of the way.

"What is it?" The moment Julianne said the words, Brody saw a figure wearing black running away from the parking lot, toward the back of the restaurant.

Reacting instinctively, he grabbed Julianne's arm. "We have to get out of here now!"

They'd gotten a good ten yards from the SUV when a loud explosion rocked the earth, sending them tumbling to the pavement.

He rolled over, raking his gaze over the scene. The FBI vehicle was on fire. Restaurant patrons leaving the building screamed and ran away from the restaurant.

Where was the guy dressed in black?

"Thunder! Heel!" Julianne's panicked voice had him searching frantically for the dog.

Thunder came running from behind the back of the building heading straight for Julianne. Brody was relieved the dog was all right, and wondered if the guy once again had a getaway vehicle to flee the scene.

"What do you have there, boy?" Julianne asked, struggling to her feet.

It took Brody a minute to realize there was a bit of fabric caught in the dog's mouth.

Thunder had been close enough to get a piece of the perp, but once again, the guy had evaded capture.

Grimly, Brody knew that this was only the beginning. They'd see this assailant again. There was no mistaking the fact that he and Julianne had been the main target of this guy's attack.

All trails leading back to Nate's jailbreak.

THREE

Julianne swept her gaze over the area, grappling with their near miss.

Someone had tried to kill them. Her and Brody, specifically.

"I'm glad Thunder managed to bring back a clue."

Brody's comment helped her focus. She still held the ripped piece of fabric in her hand, the one Thunder had brought to her. Pulling an evidence bag out of her pocket, she quickly placed the scrap of fabric inside and sealed it shut.

Then she dropped to her knee, placed her arm around the dog's neck, and gave him a hug and a treat. "Good boy."

Thunder let out his musical howl, making her smile.

"The guy must have planted a bomb under your SUV," Brody continued grimly. "If your dog hadn't alerted us to the danger..." He didn't need to finish his thought.

"Thunder has saved my life more times than I can count." Rising to her feet, she scrutinized the area around the restaurant. Thankfully, it appeared no one else was hurt, the waitress was crying, but as far as Julianne could tell, she wasn't bleeding. The picnic table Brody had chosen was covered in black soot from the fire, but seemed to be the only damage to the restaurant itself. Her vehicle wasn't parked too close to other cars, although there was a yellow pickup truck with broken windows as a result of the blast. "I don't see anyone with injuries, and there doesn't appear to be much damage, other than to my car and the yellow truck parked close by. We were fortunate."

This time.

Brody nodded, phone in hand. She listened as he called dispatch to let them know about the bomb and subsequent fire.

"How did he find us?" she asked, when he'd finished his call. "We came in two different vehicles and at two different times. I know I wasn't followed."

"Me, either. But it's a good question," Brody admitted. "Could be they just happened to drive past and noticed the K-9 logo on the back of your SUV. K-9s aren't common around here."

"Maybe. But how did they know it was mine? Max has one, too." She didn't like it. Surely the gunman she'd injured had made a point of getting away from here. Why bother to stick around?

Unless he knew about the roadblocks and decided to seek revenge. Given the history between Nate and Brody, revenge seemed plausible, but she couldn't help thinking there was something else keeping Nate around. Unfinished business? Maybe.

A short round guy with short gray hair wearing an apron over cotton pants and a T-shirt came rushing outside. He paused, giving the waitress a hug, then made his way over to them.

"Sheriff, what happened? What's going on?"

"Joe Clancy, this is FBI Agent Julianne Martinez. Julianne, this is Joe Clancy. He and his wife own Rusty's now." Brody paused, then sighed. "I'm sorry about this, Joe. I have reason to believe Agent Martinez and I were the intended targets. Don't worry, it looks like only the cars next to Julianne's were damaged, not your restaurant."

"Looks like my truck has broken windows, but I guess that's what insurance is for, right, Sheriff?" Joe blew out his breath in a heavy sigh, taking the attack on his property better than she'd anticipated. He ran his hand over his hair. "It could be worse. I'm glad no one's been hurt."

"Me, too. How's your waitress?" Julianne asked. "She was the only other person in close proximity to the blast. Might be best if she went to get checked out in the ER."

"She has a few bruises from landing on the ground," Joe said. "I think she's more scared than hurt."

Julianne didn't blame her. The incident had shaken her, too. Just standing here in plain view was making her nervous. What if the guy who'd set the bomb came back? She and Brody being here could very well be placing innocent lives in danger. Sirens wailed, indicating help was on the way. "We need to leave, Brody."

"I hear you." He turned to the restaurant owner. "Joe, Deputy Hanson is on his way to take over for me. He'll file a police report that you can submit to your insurance company."

Joe Clancy nodded and lumbered over to where the waitress still stood, wiping at her eyes.

"Do you need to stay until your deputy arrives?"

Brody shook his head. "For now, it's probably best if we stick together."

She couldn't argue his logic. Besides, there wasn't time to worry about it, they were expected to meet up with Max West at the chopper. "We'll need to take your truck, since mine is toast. I'm also going to need to replace Thunder's equipment that was inside. Thank goodness I still have the evidence bag with Jake's shirt in my backpack." The thought of losing one of their key leads made her stomach clench. This incident only proved she needed to keep the evidence with her at all times.

"Sure." Brody led the way to his SUV, with the words *Clover County Sheriff* painted across the side. He automatically went to the driver's side door, then hesitated. "Okay if I drive?"

"Yes, of course." The Brody she knew wouldn't have bothered to ask. Why was he being so open-minded now? Had he changed in other ways, too? Probably, but she told herself it didn't matter.

The bottom line was that Brody hadn't cared about her. He hadn't trusted her.

Hadn't believed in her, the way she'd needed him to.

Brody was a part of her past, not her future. As soon as they'd finished here, they'd both return to their respective lives.

On opposite ends of the country.

An hour later, after they'd stopped to pick up the items Thunder needed replaced, she joined Max at the designated meeting spot. The chopper arrived early, which suited her just fine.

Julianne wanted very badly to find Jake Morrow and knew that it was highly likely the hidden house in the woods belonged to the Duprees. Several weeks ago, after a shoot-out at a desolate warehouse, the kingpin Reginald Dupree had been arrested, but unfortunately, his second-in-command, Angus Dupree, had gotten away with Jake Morrow as his hostage. Jake's K-9 partner, Buddy, had been injured but had thankfully recovered. Their team was desperate to find Jake, worried Angus would attempt to force Jake to provide inside information. Or, worst case scenario, ask for a trade: Jake's life in exchange for letting Reginald Dupree go.

Each member of the team knew that freeing Reginald from custody was not an option.

"Zeke, this is Julianne Martinez and Sheriff Brody Kenner." Max performed quick introductions.

"I appreciate being brought in as part of the team," Zeke Morrow said, his expression solemn. He was tall, broad-shouldered with dark brown hair and dark eyes, and his partner, Cheetah, was a beautiful Australian shepherd with a black-and-white coat, mostly white around the animal's neck and chest. Julianne found herself sending up a silent prayer that they'd find Zeke's half brother alive and well.

"We're glad to have you," Max assured him.

Julianne echoed the sentiment, then tugged Max's arm. "There's an incident I need to tell you about."

Her SAC's expression turned grim. "Now what?"

"Somebody planted a bomb under my SUV while Brody and I were grabbing dinner at Rusty's, one of the restaurants located outside of town."

Max looked at Brody, then turned back to her. "A bomb?"

"Yeah. Thunder alerted us to the danger, and I happened to catch a glimpse of someone running away from the parking lot, toward the back of the building," Brody said. "We managed to get away unscathed."

"Thunder saved our lives," Julianne added. "He alerted us to the danger. We caught a glimpse of someone running toward the building, and it's likely he triggered the bomb early. Thankfully, no one else was hurt."

Max leveled Brody a stern look. "This latest development is related to your prison break, isn't it?"

"I think so, yes. I know this mission to find your agent is top priority but as soon as we've checked out the cabin, I'd like Julianne and Thunder's help in tracking our escapee. When I checked in, the deputies manning the roadblocks hadn't seen any sign of him, so that means he either slipped away or is seeking revenge against me personally for bringing him down. Based on the bomb, I'm figuring it's the latter. I'm concerned about placing more innocent lives at risk."

"Good idea. Better to go on offense rather than remaining on defense."

Brody grinned at the football analogy and Julianne remembered how they'd loved to watch college football games on Saturdays. She lived in Montana now, and they had a college team but she still followed Texas A&M, her favorite.

Did Brody still watch them, too? A bittersweet longing swept over her. She missed what they'd shared.

She missed him. At least the way he'd been before Lilly's disappearance.

"Thanks," Brody said. "Now, let's check the equipment, make sure we're ready to roll."

Once Brody was assured that they had everything they needed to parachute successfully into the Dupree compound, Max spread out a topographical map on the hood of his SUV so he could outline the plan.

"According to Dylan's estimate, this is where the house is." He drew the outline with a felt tip marker. "To the southwest, there's a small clearing, here." He made additional marks on the map, then glanced up at them. "This is our target landing zone."

"Looks like there are a lot of trees." Julianne kept her tone matter-of-fact. "How big is the landing area?"

"Roughly twenty by twenty."

"That's feet, not yards," Brody pointed out. "Y'all know it won't be easy, but it's doable. Are you sure we all need to do this? Do you need anyone to stay behind?"

"The four of us are going," Max said, gesturing to include Julianne, Zeke and Brody. "And the three dogs. That's nonnegotiable."

"Okay, I'll have my deputies on the ground, surrounding the area as backup. You, Zeke and Julianne will have to drop in carrying your dogs." Brody flashed a reassuring smile at Max. "I'm sure we'll be fine, especially since your team has done this before."

"We have." Julianne glanced down at Thunder, glad to have him as her partner. She depended on the animal to back her up, sensing danger the way he had outside of Rusty's. Besides, she needed Thunder's evidence-retrieving expertise in following Jake's scent so they could find him. She'd stuffed the bag containing Jake's shirt into her small backpack so they'd have it within the compound.

"When are we going airborne? Soon?" Zeke was clearly anxious to get going.

"Yeah." Max nodded, glancing up at the sky. "Dusk isn't as good as going in at night, but since we have everything ready to go, I don't want to wait any longer."

"Good." Julianne was relieved, she didn't particularly want to wait, either.

Time was their enemy.

Brody helped Julianne into the chopper, wishing there was a way to convince her to stay behind, far away from the heart of danger. Logically, he knew she was a well-trained, capable FBI agent, but on a personal level, he couldn't stand the idea of anything happening to her.

The only good part of this entire scenario was that he'd be down there, with her. Close at hand if she needed backup.

If he were honest, he'd admit that she was the main reason he'd insisted on coming along in the first place. He figured between him and Thunder, they'd keep her safe.

He assisted Julianne with her harness. Thunder was remarkably calm despite being airborne in a noisy chopper. Clearly they had done this before.

For the first time since seeing Julianne again, he wondered what it would be like to have a K-9 partner. He'd always thought the animals were a bit overrated, but after the way Thunder had alerted them to the impending danger, he realized he hadn't given the four-legged officers enough credit.

Their skills were amazing.

Clearly, Julianne had done well for herself. It hurt to realize that leaving him had been the right thing for her to do, in so many ways.

And he only had himself to blame.

At the time, he'd been determined to keep searching for Lilly, not just because Nate asked him to, but because he wanted to prove to Julianne that she was wrong.

He hadn't anticipated she'd turn her back on him and walk away.

He shook off the troublesome thoughts. Glancing at Julianne, he gave her a thumbs-up. The rotors of the chopper were too loud to allow conversation, although they could communicate through their headsets. The only problem was that everyone on board could hear what they said to each other.

Maybe once this was over, they'd have time to speak privately and finally put the past to rest.

"ETA five minutes." The pilot's voice came through the intercom.

Their mission was a go. Brody edged over to the door, filled with a sense of urgency fueled by adrenaline. This was it. They'd be jumping two at a time. He and Julianne would go first, followed by Max and Zeke.

Julianne bent down and lifted Thunder into her arms.

The dog's front paws went over her shoulders and she held his hindquarters firmly against her. Brody secured the strap, holding the dog in place. With a brief nod, he pushed the door open. Holding up his hand he counted down from five.

Four. Three. Two. One.

Julianne and Thunder went first; he jumped shortly thereafter.

The most difficult part of the mission was to make sure they landed in the appropriate spot. Getting their chute tangled up in the trees would be catastrophic.

Brody concentrated on steering his parachute in the appropriate direction. Julianne was directly in front of him. Thunder didn't bark or growl during the parachute ride, which was reassuring.

The ground rushed up to meet them and when a gust of wind hit hard, he cranked on the leads to stay on course.

His heart thundered in his chest. What if Julianne didn't have the strength to make the adjustment?

He dropped onto the twenty-by-twenty landing spot, his left knee jarring a bit from the force of his feet meeting the earth. He didn't waste a second, but quickly gathered the parachute into a ball, ducking out of the way to make more room as Julianne and Thunder descended, landing a few feet away.

He found himself thanking God for their safety, despite the fact that he hadn't prayed in a long time.

Without speaking, he shucked his harness. Then he stepped forward to assist Julianne and Thunder. Holding his weapon ready, he led the way to the side of the clearing and took shelter behind the largest tree. There was a faint path through the woods, leading to what he assumed must be the house.

The structure wasn't easy to see because the dark wood blended in with the surrounding foliage.

"Do you think they heard the chopper?" Julianne asked, coming up to stand beside him.

"Probably. I'm hoping whoever is here assumes that the chopper belongs to the Red River Army Base. It's roughly sixty miles to the east and it's not uncommon for choppers to come and go." Brody returned his gaze to the path. "How many guards do you expect?"

Julianne shrugged. "Four or five on the outside, but I'm sure there are a lot more inside."

He scowled, realizing he should have asked more questions about the Duprees and what they were capable of. He didn't like being outnumbered.

Having deputies surrounding the compound wouldn't be very helpful if they couldn't get inside.

Soft thuds signaled the arrival of Max, Opal, Zeke and Cheetah. Five minutes later, they came over to join them.

"We'll split up," Max directed. "Julianne, I want you and Kenner to go in from the right. Zeke and I will cross over to cover the other side."

It was on the tip of Brody's tongue to ask that Julianne stay back with Zeke while he and Max went in first, but he managed to hold back.

With four to five outside guards, it probably didn't matter one way or the other.

He and Julianne gave Zeke and Max time to make their way around the property so they could approach the house from the other side. After an excruciating ten minutes, he nodded at Julianne.

"Our turn."

He crept along the path, moving silently through the brush. Julianne and Thunder covered his back.

When they'd gone about fifty feet, he paused and took

out a pair of binoculars. The structure was closer now, just another forty to fifty yards away.

He caught a glimpse of one guard near the front door. If there were others, they were too well hidden for him to see. But he suspected there was at least one more, patrolling the perimeter.

"Found one," he whispered, handing her the binoculars. "At the door. He's not even trying to hide, but maybe there are others."

Julianne handed the glasses back to him. "Seems awfully quiet. I expected the chopper to garner some attention."

Brody didn't disagree. Even if the guards assumed the chopper belonged to the army base, which was located near the border of Texas and Arkansas, wouldn't they at least come out to make certain?

"Ready?" He looked at Julianne who nodded. "Let's go."

He shook off a wave of apprehension and moved forward. They covered another twenty yards, the house now dangerously close, when he signaled for her to wait.

Raising the binoculars again, he could see the single guard near the front door as clearly as if the guy were standing right in front of him. He was dressed in army green, with a rifle slung over his shoulder, but he also lounged against the wall of the house as if he were bored out of his mind.

Something about this wasn't right. He took his time, carefully checking the vicinity for others who might be hiding nearby.

Nothing.

Could this Dupree guy Julianne was tracking be that arrogant? Did he really think the thick woods and the fence offered him enough protection?

If so, maybe this wouldn't be as dangerous as Brody had feared.

With the guy leaning up against the wall, he couldn't go in to take him from behind. But Brody could rush him, bringing him down before he had a chance to pull his weapon.

"I'll take the guy at the door," he said using the mic to make sure Max and Zeke knew the plan. "I need everyone else to keep alert in case there are other guards who may come running."

"Roger," Max replied. Julianne simply nodded and moved a few feet ahead, putting herself and Thunder in position.

With stealthy precision Brody moved from one tree to the next, coming up on the guy's right-hand side. The gun was slung over his right arm, so Brody had to assume he was a lefty.

He rushed the guard, hitting him hard and taking him to the ground with a muffled thump. He pressed the guy's face into the earth so that he couldn't shout for assistance. But it didn't matter because within seconds the front door swung open and a second guard appeared in the doorway, his weapon pointed directly at the spot where he'd left Julianne.

Crack! Crack!

Two shots echoed through the trees. Brody's heart slammed to an abrupt stop in his chest. The guard in the doorway fell backward into the house from the force of Julianne's shot.

Brody yanked on the guard's arms, pulling them behind his back to cuff him when more gunfire rang out. The guard tried to head-butt him, so he was forced to hit back, knocking him unconscious. Then he finished tying the guy's wrists behind his back and his ankles together so the guy couldn't escape.

When he rose to his feet, he saw that Max, Zeke and

Julianne were huddled near the front door. Unfortunately, it looked as if the gunfire had been exchanged both ways; there was a bit of blood on Zeke's arm and two guards, he'd been right about one patrolling the perimeter, were dead, leaving only one to question once they'd cleared the house. Max and Zeke quickly took control of the fallen guard's weapons.

"Ready to go inside?" Max asked in a low, urgent tone. "I'll take the lead."

Julianne nodded and pulled out the same evidence bag she'd used earlier that day, the one with Jake Morrow's shirt inside. She opened the bag. Thunder buried his nose inside, taking his time to imprint the scent.

"Find Jake."

Thunder put his nose to the ground, but Julianne kept her hand on his collar, giving him a hand signal of some sort. The dog stood at her side, his nose twitching with the need to follow the scent.

Max approached the door first, taking the right side. Zeke came up on the left. After a moment they both disappeared inside, each heading in opposite directions.

Julianne stepped up to the doorway, following Max. Brody didn't like being separated from her, but took the left, following Zeke and Cheetah.

The house was plush, with at least a dozen different rooms, but there was no sign of a captured agent.

In fact, there wasn't anyone at all. Other than the three guards they'd taken care of, the place was empty.

Julianne couldn't believe that Angus Dupree and his henchmen had gotten away. Frustrated, she let go of Thunder's collar. "Find, Thunder. Find Jake."

Her partner went to work, nose to the floor, instantly alerting in the main living area. But then he kept going, down the hallway to one of the bedrooms, where he alerted again.

In the kitchen. The bathroom. Another bedroom.

Thunder found evidence of Jake in nearly every room in the entire house.

"He was here," Julianne said, glancing at Zeke. "Probably recently. We must have just missed them."

"Julianne, come look at this," Max called from one of the back bedrooms.

"What did you find?"

His expression was grim. "Blood. Fresh blood along the side of the desk chair."

She sucked in a harsh breath. "Thunder, heel."

The dog bounded to her side.

"Find Jake," she repeated. He'd already alerted in this room, but over by the side of the bed, not the desk.

Thunder put his nose to the floor, sniffing along the edge of the desk. When he got to the side where the blood was, he alerted again.

"We'll need to test the blood to match Jake's DNA, but according to Thunder it's likely his." She glanced around the room. "Maybe this is where they kept him locked up, either at the desk or on the bed."

"That's the picture I'm getting." Max opened the desk drawers, but they were empty.

Julianne went down on her knees to look under the bed. A flash of silver caught her eye. "Thunder, find Jake."

The dog crawled on his belly beneath the bed, emerging a moment later with something in his mouth. Julianne gently pried it out of his jaw.

"What is it?" Max asked.

Zeke and Brody came into the bedroom. Zeke took one look at the item she held in her hand and asked, "Where did you find that?"

"Under the bed." She looked at the heavy silver watch. "Do you recognize it?"

Zeke paled, his expression full of anguish as he nodded. "It belongs to Jake."

"How do you know?"

Zeke took the watch and turned it over. "See here? I had it engraved."

J: Proud to be your brother—Z.

She swallowed hard, handing the watch back to Zeke. "The evidence proves Jake was here."

"Yeah, but where is he now?" Zeke demanded, jamming his fingers through his hair. "And what's with the blood? Are they torturing him in order to make him talk?"

Julianne shook her head, feeling helpless. She didn't know where Dupree had taken Jake, or why there was blood on the edge of the desk.

The news didn't bode well for Jake's safety.

And worse, they were back to square one.

FOUR

"Okay, now what?" Zeke demanded, staring at Max. "You must have some idea of what our next move should be. We have to find Jake before Dupree kills him."

Brody remained silent, feeling the same frustration as the rest of the FBI team. The loss of their agent was clearly taking a toll, especially on Jake's half brother. Zeke looked mad enough to take on the world.

He couldn't blame the guy. He'd feel the same way in his shoes.

"We need an evidence team to come in and sweep this place, make sure we haven't missed anything," Max said. "And we'll take the guard into custody, see if we can get him to talk."

Zeke scowled. "You're assuming he knows something worth telling us."

"Zeke." Julianne rested a hand on the newest agent's arm in an attempt to calm him. "At this point, we'll take every bit of information we can get. Have faith, we'll find your brother."

Brody knew that Julianne's faith was strong, while his had wavered over the years. Once again, he hated the idea that she was clearly better off without him. Their disagreement over Lilly's disappearance as well as her bluntly negative opinion of Nate, had created a rift between them wider than the Mississippi River. Besides, as much as he felt bad for the FBI's missing agent, he had a bigger problem to contend with.

Finding Nate Otwell and the gunman who'd assisted his escape.

"We'd better get outside," Brody interjected. "We'll need to get the guard airlifted out of here, along with the rest of us."

"Yeah." Max jammed his fingers through his short blond hair before turning and heading back through the house, Opal at his side.

The two guards they'd been forced to shoot in self-defense were of course lying where they'd left them. But when Brody looked over to the side of the house where he'd tied up the guard he'd bound and left unconscious, the guy was nowhere to be found.

"Where did he go?" Zeke demanded.

Good question. Looking closer, Brody noticed that one of the dead guards' bodies had been disturbed. Had the guy managed to roll over here to get access to a knife? "I bound his wrists and his ankles, but he may have managed to get ahold of a knife. Still, he couldn't have gone far."

"Let's see if any of the dogs can pick up his scent," Max instructed.

Julianne took Thunder over to the spot on the ground where the bound guard had been. She pointed with her finger. "Find, Thunder. Find."

Thunder took his time sniffing the area, then trotted off toward an area of dense brush, where the branches were broken as if someone had recently barged through.

"We'll go in at another angle," Max said.

Brody battled a wave of guilt as he followed Julianne

and Thunder. He wanted desperately to find this guy. If the guard managed to escape, it would be his fault.

Just like Nate's return to his criminal past was. If he hadn't gone into the army…but he had.

So far, he hadn't exactly been much of an asset to Julianne and Max's case. Granted, the FBI agents had also searched the fallen guards for weapons, but he still felt responsible.

Thunder stopped for a moment, alerting on the base of a tree. Brody wondered if the guard had paused there to catch his breath.

"Good boy," Julianne praised. "Keep going, Thunder." She opened a bag of leaves for him to sniff. "Find."

In the brief moment of silence, the sound of a tree branch cracking echoed loudly. Brody instantly spun north. Thunder reacted at the same time, heading in the same direction from where the sound had come.

Brody clung protectively close to Julianne. She wasn't his responsibility anymore, but he couldn't seem to help himself. She was still important to him, even after all this time.

He didn't see how the guard could have gotten ahold of a gun, but he wasn't willing to take any chances. For all he knew, they had weapons stashed somewhere on the property.

Sure enough, a loud boom echoed through the air, something hitting a tree branch above their heads. He jerked her arm, covering her body with his. "Get down."

Julianne dropped to her knees as he fired back, hoping to make the guard seek cover. He knew very well Max and Zeke wanted to capture the guard alive, in order to question him.

There was more movement in the trees off to the east,

and Brody was hopeful that Max and Zeke were also hot on the guy's trail.

"Get up," Julianne whispered, pushing him out of the way so she could stand. "We need to keep going, to help box him in."

Brody didn't want her anywhere near this guy, but he held his tongue. Silently, he prayed for God to keep them all safe.

Another boom rent the air, followed closely by a second shot. He instinctively stepped in front of Julianne, but there was no indication the bullet had come in their direction.

"I hit him," Zeke shouted. "Fetch, Cheetah!"

He headed toward the sounds of Julianne's teammates. By the time they reached the guard lying on the ground, the other two FBI agents and their K-9 partners were already there.

"He's dead," Max said in a grim tone. "Shot in the head."

"I didn't aim to kill," Zeke protested. "See the wound in his thigh? That was where I hit him."

"Then what happened?" Julianne demanded.

Max slowly rose to his feet. "Looks like he shot himself in the head, rather than risk being captured."

For several long moments, they all simply stood there as the grim reality sank deep.

What kind of power did Dupree wield over his men that this guard would rather shoot himself than allowing himself to be interrogated?

And what did that say about Jake Morrow's ability to get out of this mess alive?

The next morning, Julianne woke up feeling groggy. They hadn't gotten out of Dupree's house until well after midnight. Brody would be there around nine to pick her up for breakfast, so she dragged herself upright, smiling as Thunder simply lifted his head without moving from his place on the floor next to her bed.

"Come on, Thunder, we have more work to do."

Her foxhound slowly rose and stretched languorously. Then he trotted over to the door, looking at her over his shoulder as if to say hurry up, already.

After snapping on his leash, she took him outside the small motel she and Max were staying in. Once Thunder took care of business and she finished cleaning up after him, she returned indoors. She filled Thunder's food and water bowls then quickly took a shower and dressed in a clean casual uniform, khaki pants and a short sleeved polo with the K-9 logo on the upper left pocket.

At 0900 hours, she and Thunder stepped outside the motel room at the exact same moment Brody pulled his SUV into a parking space a few spots down from her doorway. When Brody slid out from behind the wheel, dressed sharply in his brown sheriff's uniform, she was reminded that a big part of the reason she hadn't slept well had been because she'd been taunted by memories of how close they'd once been.

Of how much she'd once loved him.

Before he'd pushed her away, choosing to stay here in Clover supposedly to help his buddy Nate Otwell find Lilly, instead of joining the FBI academy with her. Brody had refused to consider the possibility that Nate had something to do with Lilly's disappearance, focusing instead on the runaway angle.

It still hurt that Brody hadn't put any faith in her opinion. That he hadn't trusted her. He and Nate had been best friends since their juvie days, but hadn't their relationship meant more to him?

Obviously not.

Over and done with, she reminded herself. Sure, she cared about what happened to him the same way she cared about all of her friends in law enforcement, but that was it. Nothing more.

So why was her heart thumping wildly in her chest every time he came near?

Memories, that's why. Julianne took a deep breath, and remained where she was, forcing Brody to come toward her.

"How are you?" he asked, his blue eyes raking over her as if she'd been injured.

She flushed, far too aware of his penetrating gaze. Granted, she had a few bruises from the activity the night before, but nothing serious. Zeke had been the one who'd been grazed by a bullet. Thankfully, his injury was nothing more than a flesh wound.

"Fine." She willed her heart rate to return to normal, glancing over to the room next to hers. "When we're finished Max wants to debrief."

Brody shook his head. "There's no time. I received a call from dispatch while I was on my way over. We have a report of bloody towels left behind in a motel room, a place called the Broke Spoke Motel. It's off Highway T about twenty miles from here."

"From our injured gunman?" she asked, trying to rein in her excitement. This would be a huge help: the towels would hopefully provide a decent scent for Thunder.

"It's possible," Brody agreed. "I figured you'd want to come with me to check it out."

"Absolutely." She didn't hesitate for a second. The guy had already tried to kill her twice; the sooner they could get hot on his trail, the better. "Just give me a minute to let Max know we're leaving."

Brody gave Thunder a pat on the head, then fell into

step beside her as she crossed over to rap on Max's door. After a few minutes, Max greeted them. "Come in. As soon as Zeke arrives, we'll start."

"Actually, we can't stay. Brody has a lead on the gunman."

Max raised a brow. "That's good news."

"We're going to head over to check it out, but I also need to know the status on my replacement vehicle." She felt bad asking, knowing that headquarters wouldn't be too happy about losing a car, but it was hardly her fault she'd been in the wrong place at the wrong time.

Max grimaced. "I'm working on it. The office in Houston isn't thrilled, but they've agreed to provide something for you during the duration of your stay here in Clover."

"Good. Any idea when I'll be able to get the keys?" It wasn't so much that she needed her own set of wheels, but she was desperate to avoid spending too much one-on-one time with Brody. Working this closely to him only reminded her of how much she'd lost when they'd broken up.

How much his refusal to choose her over Nate still hurt.

"Zeke and I can pick it up later today when we drop off the evidence we've gathered so far," Max said. "The Houston office is going to ship everything we have to the lab in Quantico."

"Would you be willing to send my evidence, too?" Brody asked. "Our state lab is severely backed up, and I need all the help I can get to find my escapee and the gunman who assisted in breaking him out."

Max shrugged. "Sure, why not? Julianne is a witness, so finding them helps our team, as well."

"Great, give me a minute and I'll bring everything in."

Brody left to return to his car, leaving Julianne and Max alone for a moment.

"How's Zeke?" she asked quietly.

"As good as can be expected." Max watched Brody, then turned toward her. "If you need help with Kenner, let me know."

She couldn't help but smile. "Don't worry, I can handle him."

"Yeah, well hurry up and put this case to rest, okay? In the meantime, I'll work with Zeke and Dylan to see if we can come up with additional information. I'm hoping that identifying the guards at Dupree's compound will give us something to go on."

"Sounds like a plan." Julianne stepped aside, giving Brody room to hand off the evidence he wanted processed.

When he'd finished, she and Thunder accompanied him to the SUV.

Silence thickened as the vehicle rolled along the highway. Julianne had hoped to avoid rehashing the past, but it seemed there wasn't much else to discuss.

"Did you ever find out what happened to Lilly Ramos?" she finally asked, bringing up the one subject that had started the rift in their relationship.

Brody's expression hardened, and he shook his head. "No. I've kept her on our list of missing persons, but everyone else in this town believes she up and ran away."

Julianne scowled. "You know as well as I do that Lilly wouldn't have run away without telling me. We were best friends, Brody. The four of us—me, you, Nate and Lilly. We double-dated all the time. What possible reason did she have to take off without leaving so much as a note?"

Brody blew out his breath in a heavy sigh. "I don't know. Lilly disappeared six months before graduation, and I'm confident Nate didn't go back to his old ways until I left him here alone, to join the army, which was eight months after we graduated."

Julianne didn't necessarily agree. "You really think that

Nate returned to his life of crime because you weren't here to keep him on the straight and narrow?"

"Yeah, I do." Brody's blunt tone contained a hard edge.

"So you think Nate's crimes are your fault." Couldn't he see how wrong that was?

"Not exactly," he reluctantly admitted. "He chose to hang out with the old crowd. Partially because I wasn't here. But maybe because he wanted easy money, too."

She could easily believe that—Nate Otwell had always seemed to prefer looking for quicker ways to make a buck, rather than working hard to get what he wanted. Hadn't she warned Lilly that Nate might not be as nice as he seemed?

But Lilly hadn't listened, claiming she loved him. Then she disappeared. Brody believed Lilly's parents when they claimed their daughter had researched Houston on her computer, that she'd run away rather than telling Nate they were through. But Julianne still thought that Nate had something to do with Lilly's disappearance. Either their friend had found out something about Nate and had run off, or she'd told him they were over, and Nate didn't like it, finding a way to shut her up for good.

No point rehashing the past, she told herself sternly. Right now, she needed to stay focused on finding Otwell. And the gunman.

The Broke Spoke Motel was a completely run-down establishment sitting right off to the east of the highway. Julianne had no problem believing that the injured gunman had been able to get a room without anyone asking any questions. It appeared the motel catered to a rough crowd.

The vacancy sign in the window was lit up, and Julianne was grateful she had a better place to stay. Not that the Clover Inn was a four-star motel by any means, but this place barely ranked one star.

And even that was being kind.

She slid out of the passenger seat and went around to open the back to let Thunder out. After snapping on his leash, she rounded the vehicle to join Brady.

"What do you have?" she asked, noticing the evidence bag in his hand.

"I stopped by the jail to get one of Nate's T-shirts," Brody explained. "I know you have that bit of cloth from the gunman, but I'm hoping Thunder can prove that Nate and the assailant are together."

"Good idea." Julianne had the bag with the bit of cloth Thunder had brought back after chasing the gunman. She opened the bag and held it out for Thunder.

"Find, Thunder. Find."

Thunder buried his snout in the bag for a moment, then wheeled around to put his nose to the ground. Julianne let her partner take the lead as he followed a trail toward the line of motel rooms that only he could see. Or smell.

Thunder sniffed along the base of the motel room doors, coming to an abrupt stop at room number six. He walked back and forth, jerked his head to the side, scratched at the ground then sat down on his rump right in front of the door.

"That must be the one," Julianne said with satisfaction.

"Let's get the manager." Brody lightly snagged her arm, steering her toward the lobby/office.

The manager was an old guy with a large belly hanging over his belt and a filthy cowboy hat on his head. When Brody flashed his badge, the guy quickly handed over the key.

"I don't want any trouble, Sheriff," he drawled. "I run a clean business. When I heard on the news you was lookin' for some guy who'd been wounded in a shoot-out, I called right away when the maid complained about the bloody towels."

"Did you leave the room exactly as she found it?" Brody

asked, pinning the old man with a fierce glare. Julianne tried not to roll her eyes—the old man was likely to lie rather than risk Brody's wrath.

"It's okay either way," she spoke up. "If the maid started cleaning before finding the towels we just need to know what surfaces she touched."

The old man's gaze bounced between them. "Yeah, uh, okay, I'll ask Becky to come talk to you."

"Thanks." Julianne flashed a smile as Brody took the key.

"You know he's not really running a clean place, here, right?" Brody asked under his breath as they returned to room six.

"You know you can catch more flies with honey than with vinegar, right?" she countered. "You were scaring the poor guy to death. We need the truth, not something fabricated to avoid being arrested."

"Hmph." Brody gestured for her to get up against the wall, as he used the key to unlock the door.

"Thunder, heel," Julianne commanded, as Brody pushed the door open. Holding his weapon at the ready, he quickly scanned the room before crossing the threshold.

She pulled her service revolver out and went in behind, backing him up. She made sure to check behind the door, as Brody approached the bathroom.

"It's clear," he said, returning his gun to its holster. "And I found the towels."

Julianne stayed near the door. She let Thunder sniff the evidence bag again, then pointed. "Find, Thunder. Find."

Thunder dropped his nose to the floor and alerted instantly. The carpet around the bed, all the way into the bathroom where the towels were lying in a discarded bloody heap on the floor.

"Good boy." She gave Thunder a quick rub.

"Would you start again, only this time with Nate's shirt?" Brody asked.

"Of course." She took the bag with Nate's shirt and went back outside the room. The maid, Becky, was hovering outside, looking nervous.

"You wanted to see me?" she asked.

"Just to verify what you did or didn't clean in this room." Julianne gestured to room six.

"Nothing. I always clean the bathrooms first, but when I saw the bloody towels I was upset so I went to complain to Mr. Jenkins. I didn't sign up for this."

Jenkins must be the rotund man with the dirty cowboy hat. "Okay, thank you. That's all we wanted to know."

Becky bobbed her head and hurried away. Julianne wondered if the girl would tender her notice or stick with the job that likely paid little more than minimum wage. She'd been clearly shaken by the bloody towels left behind.

Not her problem, and at least now, they could dust the room for prints. Of course, cross-matching the blood on the towels to the blood found in the woods would be nice, too.

"Julianne?" Brody called.

"Coming." She opened the bag holding Nate Otwell's shirt. "Find, Thunder. Find."

Thunder took a nice long sniff, then put his nose to the ground. But he walked up and down the motel room doors without alerting on anything. When she took him inside the room, he didn't alert on anything in there, either.

"Doesn't look like Nate has been here," she told Brody, who watched Thunder with an intense gaze. "I'm sorry."

"Not your fault." Brody shrugged and glanced back at the towels. "It seems odd that the gunman didn't even try to hide his presence here, doesn't it?"

"Yes, now that you mention it…" Julianne frowned. "Obviously he must be long gone by now. The maid didn't even start to clean the room, so we should be able to get some decent fingerprints."

"I'll call a team to meet us here," Brody agreed. He made the call, then disconnected from the line, rubbing the back of his neck, his expression grim. "I don't like it, Julianne. Something is off about this. It's too easy."

She nodded, respecting Brody's cop instincts since her own gut was also screaming at her. Thunder didn't seem to be sensing any danger, though, so maybe they were over-reacting. "I get the same sense of this being a setup. Let's head outside to wait for the deputies."

Brody walked outside first, momentarily blocking Julianne's view. She sighed, annoyed with his constant attempt to protect her, when suddenly she caught a glimpse of something round that rolled quickly down the sidewalk directly toward them.

"Grenade!" Brody shouted. He scooped it up and in a graceful continuous movement swung his arm up and threw it toward the large open field located across the highway mere seconds before it exploded into tiny pieces, rocking the earth beneath their feet.

FIVE

The force of the blast sent Brody flying backward into the motel room. But instead of hitting the hard floor, he landed on top of Julianne. He heard her grunt with pain and swiftly rolled off her.

"I'm sorry, are you okay?" He ran his hands over her arms and legs, reassuring himself that she wasn't hurt.

She looked as if she was having trouble breathing, so he quickly helped her into an upright position. "Just—had— the wind knocked—out of me."

"Take it easy for a moment." He held onto her with shaking hands, the close call hitting hard. What if he hadn't seen the grenade right away? They both would have been killed by the blast.

For a moment, Julianne leaned against him as if seeking strength. He held her close, burying his face in her long dark hair, reveling in the honeysuckle scent. This was what he'd missed in the years they'd been apart.

She was back in Clover with him at the moment, but only for the duration of the case. A case where she was in constant danger because she'd witnessed the prison break.

He couldn't bear the thought of her being hurt, or worse.

Thunder came over to lick Julianne's face, causing her

to chuckle weakly. "Good boy," she said, giving the dog a one-armed hug.

Tearing himself away from her wasn't easy, but Brody forced himself to rise to his feet. He went to the doorway, surveying the damage. A small patch of the dry grass in the field on the other side of the road was on fire, but other than that, it didn't look as if anyone had been hit. He didn't see any damaged cars on the highway either.

Julianne came over to stand beside him. "God was watching over us," she said in a low, husky voice.

"Yeah." He couldn't deny her sentiment. This entire incident could have been so much worse. "The bloody towels were nothing more than a trap."

"I know. But we had to investigate, Brody. That's our job."

"We need to search the area, see if Thunder can pick up his trail." He curled his hands into fists, wanting very badly to get the slimeball in custody.

She put a hand on his arm, squinting at the highway. "Wait a minute. See that black vehicle heading west, leaving a trail of dust behind? I wonder if that's him, trying to get away."

"Let's go." Brody ran for his police vehicle, grateful Julianne and Thunder quickly followed. The gunman's truck had a huge head start, but he couldn't just sit there doing nothing.

He flipped on the red and blue lights on his SUV and planted his foot on the accelerator. The motor revved, and while he didn't intend to drive recklessly, he pushed the speed as high as he dared, bound and determined to catch this perp.

But it was no use. After fifteen miles, they came upon a four-way intersection in the road. Craning his neck, he looked at each stretch of road in sequence, searching for a sign of a black vehicle, but without success. There were rusty white cars, red pickup trucks and several other types of vehicles.

But none he could pin as the black truck they'd been following.

The jerk was probably hiding in plain sight, he thought with a snarl.

Should he have Julianne work with a police artist, to get a sketch of the guy out in the public's eye?

Maybe.

His radio squawked. "Sheriff?"

He recognized Rick Meyer's voice. "Yeah, go ahead, Rick."

"We're approaching the motel, but I can see a small grass fire across the road."

"I'll call the fire department and meet you at the motel." He clicked the radio off then turned it on again. "Dispatch, send a fire truck to the Broke Spoke Motel off Highway T to contain a small grass fire."

"Will do."

He made a U-turn and headed back toward the Broke Spoke. They arrived shortly before his deputies and his guys went to work, gathering evidence and dusting for fingerprints.

Thunder had alerted them to the fact that the gunman had been there, but he was hoping to get an ID on the perp. A strong possibility, since Brody felt sure this wasn't his first criminal offense. And if that was the case, the guy's prints would be in the system.

Julianne was on the phone with her boss and he listened to her side of the conversation.

"I'm fine, Max. Brody was in more danger than I was."

Brody scowled at her. "That's not true, if you'd gone out the door first..." He couldn't finish the thought.

She waved him away. "You can't pull me from the case. I'm the only eyewitness to the murder of the van driver!"

Brody crossed his arms over his chest, his feelings playing tug-of-war with his heart.

If Max pulled Julianne from the case, taking her far away from Texas, she'd be safe from harm. The last part of the plan made him happy, but the thought of her leaving so abruptly made him grind his teeth in frustration. If only...

But no, his feelings for her, whatever they might be, didn't matter. What was important was keeping Julianne safe.

At the same time, she and Thunder were his best chance of finding Nate Otwell and the gunman.

His problem, not hers. He'd just have to find a way to deal with it.

He was so lost in his thoughts he missed the last part of her conversation with Max. She disconnected from the call and slipped her mobile phone into her pocket.

"So when are you and Max heading out?" he asked matter-of-factly. "Today or tomorrow?"

She stared at him as if he'd sprouted bat ears from his head. "What are you talking about? I'm not leaving. We need to find this guy before any more innocent people are put in harm's way."

Relief warred with concern. "Listen, Julianne, it's probably safer for you to leave—"

"No," she interrupted in a hard tone. "You have to stop doing this, Brody. I'm a trained FBI agent. Once I leave Texas, I'll continue working the Dupree case until we find Morrow. This is my job, my career. If you can't handle that, then we have nothing more to say to each other."

The steely determination in her deep brown gaze made him feel like an idiot. He wasn't against having women in law enforcement.

Just Julianne.

Because despite everything that had transpired between them, he still cared about her, far more than he should.

"You're right. I'm sorry." He gave her a terse nod. "Far be it for me to stand in the way of your job." He hoped the sarcasm in his tone wasn't too obvious.

"Good."

His radio buzzed and he took the call. "Kenner."

"Sheriff? We have a report of a break-in at the Paws and Claws Veterinary Clinic. Seems there may be supplies missing, bandages and the like. Possibly even medications."

The gunman, he thought. No doubt looking for something to take care of his injury. "Thanks, we'll head right over."

"What's going on?" Julianne asked.

"A veterinary clinic outside of Clover has been broken into. It's possible that our gunman used that as a place to seek refuge and tend to his wounds in order to avoid going to a hospital?"

"Let's go," Julianne said, tugging on Thunder's leash. "Thunder will let us know if the gunman or Nate were there."

"Yeah, okay." Brody went into the room to talk to his deputies. "When you're finished here, take the evidence straight to FBI Special Agent in Charge Max West at the Clover Inn. He's going to send everything to Quantico for processing."

"Sounds good, boss," Rick said.

Dan scowled. "Nothin' wrong with the state lab, is there?"

Brody swallowed the urge to tell Hanson to get over himself. The guy's attitude had never been great, but in the past twenty-four hours Deputy Hanson had been more surly than usual. "The feds are offering their help, we'd be foolish not to take it. This is about getting Otwell and the gunman back behind bars as soon as possible. I'll check in with you later."

Julianne and Thunder were waiting for him outside, near his SUV. As he slid behind the wheel, he hoped and prayed they weren't heading into another trap.

Julianne spread her trembling hands on her legs, willing her heart rate to settle down to normal. This was nothing more than the physical response of adrenaline, after their close call.

Not at all related to the way Brody had briefly held her in his arms.

For a few seconds it was as if they were back in college, holding each other close as they gazed up at the stars in the deep, dark sky. She was hit by an intense longing to regain what had been shattered beyond repair six years ago.

Her father had been a cop, one of the main reasons she'd earned a degree in criminal justice, going on to win a coveted spot in the FBI academy. After she and Brody had graduated from college together, it had bothered her immensely that Lilly still hadn't contacted them or been found. After Brody hadn't believed in her enough to listen to her concerns, she'd known he couldn't possibly care about her as much as she'd loved him.

Enough, she told herself. There was no point in wishing things had been different. She and Brody needed to work together in order to capture Nate and the gunman who'd helped him escape.

Their personal feelings, especially the old anger and arguments they'd had, would only be a distraction, interfering with their ability to get the job done.

Less than an hour later, Brody pulled into the parking lot of the Paws and Claws Veterinary Clinic. Julianne made sure she had both evidence bags before she let Thunder out of the back of Brody's SUV.

"The front door looks to be intact," he said, waving at it with his hand. "Let's go around to the back."

She nodded. They rounded the corner of the building. The back door, likely mostly used for supplies and employees, stood ajar, the frame dented and scarred as if someone had used their boot to kick their way inside.

"Do you think we can get a shoe print from this?" Julianne hunkered down by the door, carefully examining the muddy partial print.

"Good idea. Although it's going to take some time. All my deputies are tied up either on roadblocks or at other crime scenes."

She nodded, understanding that his Clover County resources were already stretched thin. "We may be able to get an evidence collection team here from the Houston FBI office," she told him. "That would speed things along."

To his credit, Brody didn't hesitate. She knew it couldn't be easy to invite the feds into his criminal case. "I'd appreciate any help we can get."

Julianne stood and walked away from the building to call Max. "Hey, can you smooth the way to get us assistance from the Houston office? Not just to process the evidence we've already found, but we could use additional crime scene techs to work our crime scenes."

"Scenes?" Max repeated. "As in more than one?"

"Two at the moment, with possibly more to come. Otwell and his sidekick gunman have been busy."

"Sure, no problem. I'll call the SAC in Houston. Tell me where you are."

Julianne gave her boss the name and location of the veterinary clinic. "Thanks, Max."

"Stay safe," he responded, before disconnecting the call.

Brody came over to stand beside her. "Are you and Thunder ready to go inside?"

"Yes. We'll use the gunman's scent first, since he's been injured and the one most likely to have broken in." She pulled out the evidence bag containing the small scrap of fabric Thunder had retrieved. "Find, Thunder. Find."

Thunder took a long moment to fill his head with the scent from his target, then began searching the area for the shooter's trail. He picked up the scene in the parking lot, following it around the building to the back doorway, where he alerted with a strong reaction.

"Good boy, Thunder." Julianne pushed the door open. "Find," she repeated.

Thunder continued inside the clinic, where he alerted again in the area where at least six cages were stacked. Only two were occupied, one containing a tabby cat, and another a toy poodle wearing the cone of shame to prevent him from licking his stitches.

"Will he be distracted by the animals?" Brody asked in a hushed tone.

She shook her head. Thunder was single-minded when it came to the hunt. Once she called him off, he'd probably head right over to the cages.

Thunder alerted in front of a cabinet, the broken door hanging open, the contents spewed all over the place. "The gunman was here," she said with certainty. "Looks as if he was looking for supplies and medications, but we'll need the owner of the clinic to let us know exactly what's missing."

"I'll give Clark Davenport a call. He's the veterinary assistant for Dr. Vanessa Grover. I'm sure he's the one who does the stocking."

"Good. Where is the vet by the way?" Julianne asked.

"I'm right here." A woman with reddish-brown hair liberally threaded with gray walked into the clinic, looking in dismay at the mess. "I'm Dr. Grover."

Julianne walked over to shake the woman's hand. "FBI Agent Martinez," she said, introducing herself. "I'm working with Sheriff Kenner on a case involving an escaped prisoner."

"Nate Otwell," Dr. Grover said with a nod. "I saw it on the news."

"We have an unknown gunman who facilitated his escape," Brody said, joining the conversation. "Agent Martinez wounded him and we have good reason to believe that he may be the one responsible for the break-in."

Dr. Grover scowled. "I hope you catch him, Sheriff."

Seeing the veterinary clinic reminded Julianne of the K-9 unit's mission to adopt a puppy from each area they were deployed to, as a way to both honor Jake and show the strength of their team. The puppy would be brought home to be trained as a K-9 officer. She made a mental note to ask Vanessa Grover if she knew of any puppies in need of a good home.

For now, she decided it was more important to focus on the issue at hand.

"You could help by telling us exactly what's missing from the cabinet," Julianne said, crossing over to where the broken door hung askew.

Dr. Grover sighed and shook her head. "I can tell you I keep medicine in that cabinet, and the drawers—" she pointed to the two deep drawers located to the sides of the sink "—hold various types of dressings. I don't usually do the inventory, that's Clark's job."

"But you'd have an inventory listing, wouldn't you?" Julianne pressed. "We'll talk to Clark, too, but would like whatever information you have as well."

Dr. Grover nodded. "Sure, I can pull up what I have on the computer."

"Don't use this computer yet," Brody said. "We want to dust for prints first. What time did you leave the clinic last night?"

"I left after seeing my last patient of the day, about 6:00 p.m." Dr. Grover gestured toward the two caged animals. "But Clark was going to come back around nine o'clock at night to be sure our two boarders were taken care of." The vet frowned. "Clark was also supposed to be here bright and early this morning, too. I admit I was irked when I arrived and realized he hadn't come in yet."

A prickling sensation raised the hairs on the back of Julianne's neck. She glanced at Brody, who also looked grim. "We need to call Clark, ASAP," she said.

"I know," he agreed. "Dr. Grover, will you give us his contact information?"

The vet rattled off Clark's phone number and Brody made the call. "No answer. In fact, my call went straight to voice mail."

"I don't like it," Julianne muttered, catching Brody's crystal-blue eyes with hers. "Something's not right."

"I feel the same way." He pulled out his cell and called his dispatcher. "Send a vehicle to the address of Clark Davenport," he instructed. "If found, bring him in for questioning."

"Wait a minute," Dr. Grover protested. "Clark loves working with animals and he's very responsible. There's no way in the world I'd believe he's involved in this. He would never leave our furry patients to fend for themselves."

"We're not saying he did this intentionally," Julianne told her. "You said yourself that it's strange he didn't show up for work this morning."

"Oh!" Dr. Grover put a hand over her mouth, her eyes

wide with horror. "You think the fugitive took him against his will?"

"We don't know anything yet," Julianne corrected. "Please, Dr. Grover, just let us do our job, okay? Why don't you get us that inventory list?"

"But use the computer in the main lobby area, nothing back here," Brody told her. "We'll need to make sure there aren't fingerprints on the desk."

"Yes. Okay... I'll do that." The vet walked through the doorway leading to the front of the clinic. A few minutes later, she returned with several pages. "Here, this is the medication and supply inventory. It was last reconciled last week Friday."

Julianne took the information, scanning over the long list of itemized supplies. Last Friday was five days ago, which meant it wouldn't be easy to figure out what was missing versus what had been used on the clinic's small four-legged patients.

Except...she narrowed her gaze on the list of antibiotics, then walked over to the medication cabinet. Sure enough, every single bottle of antibiotics was missing. And so were all the pain medications.

She let out a heavy sigh. Not likely that the clinic had gone through the entire inventory of antibiotics and pain meds in five days.

Brody came over to stand beside her. "The deputy at Clark's house claims he's not home and that his dog, Banjo, was locked inside the house. I'm afraid it doesn't look good. Clark Davenport is definitely missing."

"Along with all the antibiotics and pain meds," Julianne added, deeply concerned about this newest twist in the case. "I hate to say this, but I believe the gunman took them."

"Of course. The same drugs are used in animals and

people, although obviously the human doses are higher than what we normally use for pets," Dr. Grover said helpfully. "Because they're weight based."

"Would the gunman be smart enough to figure that out?" Julianne asked.

The vet blanched. "If not, Clark certainly would. Oh, dear, maybe that's why he's missing! Maybe the gunman forced Clark to go along with him to treat his injury?"

Julianne nodded slowly. The vet's theory made sense. As much as she hated to admit it, it looked as if another innocent life was in jeopardy.

How many more, she wondered. How many more innocent people would suffer before they brought Nate Otwell and the gunman to justice?

SIX

The idea of Clark Davenport being held hostage by their mystery gunman and Nate Otwell made Brody feel sick to his stomach.

It hadn't been that long ago that Brody had been forced to tell Clark that his younger sister, Renee Davenport, had been one of the young women he'd found in Otwell's cabin. Renee, along with the other four young captives, had broken down sobbing when he'd rescued them. Renee had been emotionally traumatized by her horrible experience. In fact, Clark's sister had immediately left town to live with her aunt and uncle in Houston.

Now Clark was undoubtedly suffering at Otwell's hands, too.

He couldn't help feeling resentful at the unfairness of it all. Why should one family face so much adversity? The faith, which he'd returned to since being with Julianne again, wavered.

Then he remembered hearing their church pastor reminding them not to question God's plan. It wasn't easy, but he did his best to set his emotions aside to focus on finding the gunman and Nate in time to rescue Clark.

"We need to find some usable fingerprints," he gritted out. "I need to know who this scumbag is."

"The crime scene techs from Houston will be here in thirty minutes," Julianne informed him. "I want Thunder to search for Nate's scent, too."

"Good idea." Raking a frustrated hand through his hair, he watched as Julianne took Thunder back outside. It was a good fifteen minutes later when she and Thunder returned, the dog sniffing around the clinic from one side to the other.

Nothing. Julianne sighed. "Nate wasn't here. But we know for sure the gunman was. And there's still a chance your deputies will find something at the Broke Spoke."

Brody glanced around the veterinary clinic. "The bloody towels in the motel room were nothing more than a trap. I don't think they're going to find anything useful there. But this," he said, exhaling roughly and sweeping a hand over the area, "looks like the work of someone feeling desperate. I can't help but think this is where we'll find the clues we need to pinpoint this guy's identity."

"You may be right," Julianne conceded. Thunder sat at attention by her side, and she rested her hand on his head. "We should probably head over to Clark's place."

"You think Clark was taken from his home?" Brody asked.

"I'm not sure, but I'm not ready to rule out any possibility, are you?"

Maybe not. Brody glanced around the area again. "Based on the back door being kicked open, I believe the gunman gained access to get the supplies and medications he needed, only to be interrupted by Clark when he returned to feed the animals. Because Clark found him, and because he's trained as a vet assistant, the gunman decided to take him hostage. If Clark had already been here feeding the animals, there wouldn't be a need for the gunman to bust in. Same logic if the gunman kidnapped Clark from his house to bring him here."

"Unless Clark refused to cooperate by using a key, requiring the gunman to use force to enter the building," Julianne argued. "But either way, that isn't the main reason I want to go to Clark's house. I need something with his scent in order for Thunder to track him."

"Okay." Brody glanced at his watch. "Unfortunately, I can't leave here until the crime scene techs arrive."

Julianne turned toward Dr. Grover. "Do you know how to get to Clark's?"

Brody didn't like the idea of Julianne heading over to Clark's without him, but managed to hold his tongue. It wasn't that long ago that she'd chastised him for being overprotective to the point he wouldn't let her do her job.

"I can take you there as soon as I feed the animals." Dr. Grover went over to the cages, talking to her patients in a low reassuring tone as she gave them food and water. After a few moments, the vet returned to where they waited. "I don't have any antibiotics to give Sassy, the poodle who I just operated on, yesterday," she said with a deep frown. "I need to call around to some local vets to see if anyone can sell me some supplies to hold me over until I can order more."

"If you'd rather stay here to do that, just give me the directions," Julianne said. "I'll borrow Brody's SUV and drive there myself."

"Here, I'll write them," Brody said, pulling a notebook and stubby pencil from his uniform pocket. It went against the grain to let Julianne out of his sight, but he knew she wouldn't appreciate his hovering over her. "I can't let Dr. Grover disturb anything on the desk area until the techs arrive."

Dr. Grover wrinkled her nose, but nodded her understanding. After jotting down the directions for Julianne, he handed them to her. "Call if you see anything that indicates Clark was taken by force from his home. And please be careful." His gaze clung to hers for a long moment.

"I will." Julianne flashed a wan smile and took the slip of paper. "Come, Thunder."

Brody watched them leave, glad to know that Julianne wouldn't be alone. Since he'd first heard the dog's musical howl, he'd been impressed by how well trained Thunder was and how well he protected her. And vice versa.

Leaving Julianne in Thunder's care wasn't easy. Their strained personal relationship aside, he wanted to be there with her. He forced himself to concentrate on the scene of the crime. Dr. Grover was outside making calls, so he studied the surface of the desk, unable to say for sure if anything was disturbed. Then he crossed over to examine the broken cabinet door.

There were scratches along the surface of the silver lock, as if someone had, rather clumsily, tried to jimmy it open with a sharp object. In his opinion, this gave credence to his theory that the gunman had broken in before Clark had arrived. He crouched down to look at the partially open drawer, but couldn't see any smudges that might be fingerprints on the glossy surface.

An open box of plastic gloves caught his eye, and he quickly walked over. The box looked to be brand-new; the small slit in the plastic opening along the top where gloves could be removed was narrow and had clear indentations where someone had pressed down in order to remove the gloves.

This, he thought with a surge of satisfaction. This was a good place to check for fingerprints.

"I'm so thankful for Dr. Hendrickson," Dr. Grover said

as she returned. "He's sending one of his techs over with both antibiotics and pain medications."

"Great news," Brody agreed.

"How long before I can reopen my clinic?" she asked.

Now the bad news. "Not until the techs dust for prints and see if they can find any other trace evidence, I'm afraid," Brody said regretfully. "Come over to the desk here. Does everything look the way you left it?"

She shrugged. "From what I can tell, yes." Then she frowned and leaned closer. "Wait a minute, what is that?"

"Don't touch anything," Brody warned. "Show me what caught your attention."

"There's a piece of paper shoved at an angle beneath the stack of invoices," she said, showing him the spot she meant. "I know that I went through those invoices yesterday, and I don't remember anything being underneath them."

Brody could see what she meant. The slip of paper was probably nothing, but he'd need to make sure. Using the eraser part of the pencil, he gently tugged the paper free.

Help me!

A chill snaked down his back. He glanced at Dr. Grover. "Is this Clark's handwriting?"

"Yes." Her voice was barely above a whisper. "Poor Clark."

Brody silently echoed her sentiment. There was no denying the veterinary assistant was in grave danger.

Too bad he had no idea where the gunman had taken his hostage.

Finding Clark's small house wasn't too difficult. The area had changed in the years she'd been gone, but some of the landmarks were still the same. Like the three white birch trees that formed a small triangle at the corner of the property belonging to Mr. Wilder's auto-body service center. They were taller now, slender silvery leaves seeming to reach all the way to the sky as they fluttered in the gentle breeze.

It was strange how quickly she'd become accustomed to living in Montana, the mountainous terrain so different from the sprawling landscape of Texas. The FBI K-9 headquarters building was a six-story brick building in the heart of downtown Billings. A retired FBI K-9 agent had donated a large parcel of land specifically for a K-9 training center. Being so far away from Quantico helped them keep a low profile, their missions highly confidential. She liked living there, even though much of her time was spent in other places, but being back in Clover, it suddenly hit her how much she'd missed hearing Brody's low, husky drawl.

How much she missed being home. Her parents were gone now, had died in a horrible train crash while she was at the academy, but the town still held many happy memories.

Sad and hurtful ones, too, she reminded herself. Losing Brody had been excruciating. Especially discovering he hadn't cared about her as much as she'd thought.

The deputy that had responded to look for Clark was already gone by the time she arrived, hopefully taking Clark's dog, Banjo, back to the veterinarian. Once again, she realized how short Brody was on resources. She and Thunder approached Clark's small, rather run-down home and was surprised to find the door wasn't locked.

Had Clark left it open, or had the deputy?

She pulled her 9 mm from its holster, and then carefully drew the front door open. Moving slowly, she and Thunder entered the premises.

The place was empty, without any sign of a struggle or Clark's dog for that matter. If something bad happened to

Clark, who would take care of Banjo? She'd offer to adopt him, but K-9 training had to be started when the dogs were young. Deciding to worry about that later, she opened the evidence bag with the scrap of clothing belonging to the gunman.

"Find, Thunder. Find!"

The dog sniffed around the front of the house, trotting back down to the driveway. Moments later, he returned to Julianne's side, without alerting. She let Thunder sniff around the inside of the house, too. Despite the weathered look on the outside, the interior was cozy and remarkably tidy. Julianne made her way to what she assumed was Clark's bedroom, to find a shirt or some item of clothing that hadn't been laundered. When she opened the closet door, she found a laundry basket with a white T-shirt lying inside.

She turned the evidence bag inside out so that her hand was covered, then grabbed the shirt, pulling the edges of the bag around so that it was safely tucked inside.

Thunder was still sniffing around, but she knew that Brody was right about his theory that Clark had surprised the gunman inside the veterinary clinic.

Outside, she remembered the evidence bag containing Nate's shirt. She played with Thunder, using his favorite toy, enjoying his oddly musical howl. After a few minutes she told him it was time to go back to work. She used Nate's scent, making sure that Thunder truly carried the correct scent in his nose, before issuing her command.

"Find, Thunder. Find!"

As before, Thunder put his nose to the ground, making a zigzag along the edge of the driveway before making his way up to the house. Inside, he immediately alerted in the kitchen, and again in the living room. But nowhere else.

She stood for a moment, considering the possibilities.

Could be that Nate and Clark were once friends. Nate could have been here a long time ago, maybe even before he was arrested. But that didn't seem likely, especially considering the neatness of the place. Surely the scent would have been washed away by now.

Another theory could be that Nate had come here to get Clark, forcing him to go to the clinic at gunpoint, meeting up with the gunman. But Thunder hadn't found Nate's scent anywhere around or inside the clinic.

She shook her head, frustrated that the pieces of the puzzle refused to mesh together to make a clear picture.

Sweeping one last glance around the inside of Clark's house, she turned to leave. Maybe the Houston crime scene techs could find something that would help fill the holes of their case.

By the time she returned to the veterinary clinic, the crime scene techs had begun to dust for prints. Brody and Dr. Grover stood outside, under the shade of a tall tree, Brody's frame towering over the vet. Even after all these years, she still found him incredibly attractive.

"Find anything?" Brody called out as she and Thunder approached.

She willed her heart rate to settle down, trying to hide her innate reaction to his presence. "I have one of Clark's shirts, and I had Thunder check the house for both the gunman and Nate." She held his gaze for a moment. "Thunder alerted on Nate's scent in the kitchen and living room, but gave me no indication the gunman had been there."

"Nate?" Brody repeated with a frown. "That's odd considering Thunder didn't find Nate's scent, here."

"Were they friends?"

Brody's expression turned grim. "No, in fact Clark hated Nate."

"Why?"

"Nate had lured Clark's younger sister, Renee, by getting her hooked on drugs. She was one of the victims I caught him with when I finally arrested him. He'd been in the process of selling her into a life of prostitution."

Julianne couldn't hide her gasp of outrage. "That's terrible. Still, Nate and the gunman must have split up last night. Maybe Nate went to Clark's house while he and the gunman were busy in the clinic. Although I can't say why Nate would do that."

"Money? Food?" Brody suggested.

Julianne shrugged. "Who knows? Oh, and there was no sign of Clark's dog, either. I'm assuming the deputy who'd gone over there took the dog home with him."

"I'd like to help care for Clark's dog while he's missing," Dr. Grover spoke up.

"Thank you. I'll let my deputy know," Brody assured her.

"Did you come up with anything here?" Julianne asked.

"Clark wrote two words on a scrap of paper. *Help me.*"

She winced, feeling terrible about the veterinary tech. "He must not have known where the gunman was taking him, or he would have let us know," Julianne mused. "They could be anywhere."

"I know." Brody did not look happy, and she couldn't blame him. It had been almost twenty-four hours since Nate Otwell's jailbreak, and they were no closer to finding him.

Instead, they'd been attacked twice.

She walked over to Brody's SUV, filled Thunder's water dish and set it on the ground. Her partner lapped at the bowl until it was empty.

"Good boy," she murmured, giving him an affectionate rub. She was grateful that Thunder had helped provide information to their investigation that they otherwise wouldn't have known. They made a great team.

She closed her eyes for a moment and prayed for wisdom and the strength to find Clark before he was hurt, or worse.

Her phone rang, and she quickly answered when she recognized Max's number. "Martinez."

"I left your replacement vehicle at the sheriff's department," Max informed her. "We dropped off all the evidence, including what Kenner's deputies found at the Broke Spoke. It's all being processed, ASAP."

"Good. Anything else?"

"No, but we have a lead on additional properties in the area belonging to one of Dupree's guards. In fact one of them has a younger brother. Zeke and I are heading over there to check it out."

"Keep me posted if you find anything," Julianne said.

"I will. We've checked out of the motel, and I put your suitcase in the back of your replacement vehicle. Based on the recent attack on you and Kenner, I think we should split up, keep a low profile. Too many feds in one place will only raise unwanted attention. Our mission is supposed to be classified. Bad enough that we had to bring the sheriff into our case. I don't want too many others to know the details of what we're dealing with."

"Yeah, I hear you. Talk to you later." She disconnected the line, not at all thrilled to be forced into close proximity to Brody, but she was a professional.

She'd handle it. Ignoring her tumultuous feelings for him.

It was several hours later before they received any good news.

"Agent Martinez?"

She glanced expectantly at the tech who'd called her name. "Yes?"

"We found a few nice prints on the glove box, and a partial on the edge of the broken cabinet. And we also have a partial on the boot print on the outside of the door. Looks to be a size-eleven cowboy boot with a worn tread."

"Thanks. We'd like an ID on those fingerprints as soon as possible. Please call my mobile number." Julianne gave him the numbers as he plugged them into his phone.

"Will do."

"Does this mean I'll be able to reopen my clinic?" Dr. Grover asked hopefully. "Although not sure why I'm bothering, since the day is almost over. Oh, and don't forget to let your deputy know to drop off Clark's dog."

"You'll be able to reopen soon," Brody promised. "And I've just called dispatch, the deputy is going to swing by and drop off Banjo."

Dr. Grover nodded.

He came up to stand beside Julianne. "We missed lunch and it's almost dinnertime. I'm hungry, how about you?"

She grimaced, remembering the last time they'd shared a meal. It had felt too intimate, as if they were on a date rather than two colleagues working a case. But since her stomach was growling, she acquiesced. "Yes, I'd like to eat, and to feed Thunder, but I don't like the idea of putting anyone in danger."

"We'll need a place to stay for a few days," Brody said thoughtfully. "I don't think it's smart to go back to the same motel you and your team stayed in last night."

"Max and Zeke already checked out," Julianne informed him. "My stuff is in a car parked outside your sheriff's department. You have someplace in mind?"

"There's a place called the Thoroughbred Inn, located not far from here," Brody informed her. "They have tiny kitchenettes, but it's probably best if we pick up a pizza to go."

She shrugged. "Why not?"

Another hour went by before they were checked into adjoining rooms at the Thoroughbred Inn, the surroundings luxurious compared to the Broke Spoke, but certainly nothing fancy. The kitchenette area made the rooms bigger than she'd expected. They decided to eat in Julianne's room. She filled Thunder's food and water dishes, prior to joining Brody at the table.

She bowed her head to pray. "Dear Lord, thank you for keeping us safe in Your care today. We ask that You continue to watch over Clark, to keep him safe, as well. Lastly, we thank You for this food we are about to eat, Amen."

"Amen," Brody echoed.

She couldn't help but smile, remembering how often they'd done this same thing during college. But then her smile faded. They weren't the same people they were back then, and she found herself missing the closeness they once shared.

Brody's embrace. His kisses.

"It's nice being here with you. I haven't prayed much since you've been gone," Brody said.

His admission warmed her heart, although she was disheartened by his lack of faith. "Why not?"

He shrugged. "I guess I fell out of the habit, especially after the long hours I was putting in during the investigation against Nate."

And there he was, the man who'd come between them. Her appetite waned, but she forced herself to take a bite of her pizza, topped with the works, knowing she needed to keep up her strength. She turned the conversation back to the issue at hand.

"Do you have an idea who the gunman might be?"

Brody looked surprised. "No, why would I?"

"I figured you might know who some of Nate's accomplices are."

"I arrested the guy I trailed to the cabin," Brody said. "I questioned Nate for hours, thinking I could use our former friendship to get through to him, but without success. When he asked for his attorney, the interrogation came to an end."

"Is that when you realized I was right about him six years ago?" she challenged.

He scowled. "Nate wasn't responsible for Lilly's disappearance. He didn't turn back to his life of crime until after I left him alone to join the army."

The years fell away, and they were suddenly right back to the old arguments. "And my feelings don't mean anything to you, right?"

Brody didn't respond, then again, he didn't have to. She knew the truth.

They ate in silence for a few minutes. From the way Brody avoided her gaze, she sensed he wanted her to drop the subject, but she couldn't leave it alone.

"What about the juvenile facility you and Nate attended together when you were young?" she asked, breaking the prolonged silence. "Don't you think the gunman could be one of the guys he befriended back then? One of the guys who had a criminal record?"

Brody seemed to go tense. "Like me?"

She frowned. "Of course not you. But don't you think it's likely that someone from there reconnected with Nate later? Someone who'd gone into a life of crime with him?"

"No." Brody shoved away from the table and rose to his feet in a jerky movement. "I'm not going to incriminate someone based on a slim connection from well over a decade ago. It's not fair to judge them based on some stupid stunt they pulled when they were too young to appreciate the consequences of their actions. People are considered innocent until proven guilty, remember?"

She sucked in a harsh breath. Those were the same words he'd thrown at her back when she'd accused Nate Otwell of being involved in Lilly's disappearance.

Without another word, Brody stalked through the connection between their rooms. He didn't slam the door, but shut it with a decisive click, effectively ending the conversation.

She stared down at the remains of her dinner, her appetite disappearing in a nanosecond. Brody was one of the few who'd turned his life around, and he remained touchy about his relationship with Nate and the other kids he'd met during his time in juvie. He'd always wanted to believe in their ability to do the same, turn their lives around for the better.

A noble cause, sure, but she had never liked Nate. Brody had shrugged off her concerns about him, standing up for his friend.

Time to face the truth. Brody hadn't loved her six years ago. And there was no reason to believe that had changed in the time she'd been away, either.

SEVEN

It didn't take long for Brody to regret his ridiculous behavior. What was wrong with him? Yes, he very much believed that all people should be considered innocent until proven guilty, but that wasn't the way he should have handled the situation with Julianne.

He sat on the edge of the bed and dropped his head into his hands. She'd hit a sore spot, especially dragging up their past argument, throwing her beliefs about Lilly's disappearance once again in his face.

Yet he couldn't blame her for asking the question about other kids he'd served time with. Julianne was right, the gunman could very easily be someone he and Nate had met during their time in a juvenile detention center. In fact, it was highly probable.

But what was he supposed to do? Take a wild guess? Or decide who the most likely candidate might be based on decade-old crimes that had been committed? Each one of them had come to the juvie center with a criminal background, some worse than others.

The thought of guessing wrong bothered him. He couldn't imagine ruining an innocent person's life, or wasting time going after the wrong perpetrator. No, the best approach would be to wait until the FBI lab processed the evidence, providing direction for their investigation.

Besides, if he were to be completely honest with himself, he knew it wasn't smart to trust his judgment. He'd believed Nate had turned his life around, which he had, at least initially. But after Brody left to join the army, his former friend had slipped back into his old ways, as easily as if he'd never been a law-abiding citizen for almost eight years.

Nate had damaged so many lives. Trusting him had been the absolute wrong thing to do.

He wouldn't, couldn't afford to make the same mistake again.

The sound of a door opening and closing had him jerking his head upright. Springing to his feet, he hurried over to the window, his heart thumping wildly in his chest.

He let out a sigh of relief when he realized that Julianne was only taking Thunder outside to do his business, one of the reasons he'd insisted on getting rooms on the ground level.

She wasn't leaving him.

At least, not yet.

But she would when this mission was over. And there was nothing he could do or say to stop her.

After watching her and Thunder walk along the perimeter of the building for a few minutes, he forced himself to turn away. Foolish to long for something he could never have. He'd chosen to stay behind, first to serve his country, then to serve his community.

Wishing he could go back to change the past was useless.

He stretched out on the bed, fully dressed, staring blindly at the ceiling. Where was Nate hiding out? Brody didn't think he'd return to any of his old hangouts, although he should have one of his deputies check things out to be sure.

But Nate wasn't stupid. He'd know those would be the places Brody would look. It wasn't a good thing when the criminal you were hunting knew you better than anyone else. Nate had used his friendship with Brody to his advantage, over these past few years.

Brody's gut clenched at the thought.

Despite his intent not to think about the other kids they'd served time with, he found himself going through them one by one. Billy Ray Creech. John Williamson. Kurt Royce. Jerome Fontaine. Jeff Polzin.

Soon their faces merged together in his mind, morphing into Nate's round features. Nate was the true bad guy here, and he had to admit that any one of the old crowd could be involved as well.

Apparently Brody had dozed for a bit, because the sound of a door closing had him blinking his eyes in confusion. Julianne and Thunder must have come back inside. He sat up and dragged his hand through his hair, wondering if he should go over and apologize.

Gingerly, he opened his door just enough to see if she'd locked him out, relieved to discover she hadn't. She was a strong, independent federal agent, yet no one was infallible. Thunder lifted his head, looking over at him, his tail thumping in greeting. But even then, the dog didn't move from his spot in front of the closed bathroom door. Brody smiled, glad that Thunder was there as an added source of protection for Julianne.

He backed off, leaving his side ajar in case she needed something during the night.

Returning to his position on the bed, he mentally reviewed the evidence they'd gathered so far. Fingerprints at the Broke Spoke, the veterinary clinic and Clark's house.

Blood from the woods and the motel towels. Shell casing and bullet fragment from the woods. Size-eleven cowboy boot with a worn tread from the clinic.

More than he'd anticipated, yet so far not enough to give them a hint as to who the gunman might be.

Thoughts were still running through his mind, and once again he must have fallen asleep because a dull thud similar to that of someone closing a car door brought him instantly awake. Not unusual for a motel, but he got up anyway, moving once again to the window overlooking the parking lot.

It took a minute for his eyes to adjust as he peered through the darkness. His SUV was parked around the corner, out of the immediate area, leaving the parking spaces outside his and Julianne's doors vacant.

He frowned, realizing that there wasn't any light illuminating from the small fixtures attached to the wall outside each door.

A chill snaked down his spine, filling him with a sense of apprehension. Even though it was hard to believe that the assailant had found them, he couldn't afford to take any chances.

Not with Julianne's life on the line.

Julianne bolted upright at the sound of Thunder's low growl. He was standing right in front of the door leading outside, his keen nose and hearing clearly sensing danger.

Grabbing her weapon from the nightstand, she rolled off the bed and onto her feet at the exact same moment that Brody pushed open the door between their rooms.

"Someone cut the power or took out the bulbs in each of the lights outside the doors," Brody said in a grim whisper. "We need to get out of here."

She nodded, swallowing hard. "There's only one way

out," she softly pointed out. "The gunman could be out there, waiting for us to leave, hoping to kill us as easily as ducks floating down the river."

"I know." He glanced at Thunder, then shook his head. "But we're trapped if we stay inside."

A no-win situation if she ever saw one. The thought of sending Thunder out first made her feel sick to her stomach. She couldn't bear the thought of her partner being shot.

There had to be another way. But what? Some sort of diversion? Maybe.

She turned to scan the room, racking her brain for a solution. Starting a fire was risky, but smoke would give them a bit of cover as they made their escape.

Towels might burn. She could use Thunder's metal bowl to contain the flames, but would there be enough smoke? She didn't think so.

Her gaze landed on the fire extinguisher attached to the wall in the kitchenette area. She quickly ran over and pulled it out of the holder, convinced the canister full of smoky powder would work.

"Good thinking," Brody said, admiration reflected in his gaze.

Her smile was tight as she pulled the elastic ponytail holder out of her hair and wrapped it around the handle. "Okay, here's the plan. I'll hold Thunder back while we open the door. We can use the fire extinguisher to cover us as we rush out of here."

"I'm afraid he'll just shoot at the smoke, regardless. I think it's better if we can toss it outside one door, using the other to escape. They might think it's a bomb, especially once the canister hits the pavement."

She could see his point. "All right." She pulled on her backpack, clipped Thunder's leash to his collar and tugged him back from the door. Brody took the fire extinguisher through the connection into his room. Her chest tightened with fear, and she realized how much she didn't want to lose Brody now that she'd found him again.

He pulled the locking pin, opened the door and then pressed the trigger, quickly looping the rubber band to keep it in place. Smoke erupted from the nozzle and he tossed it out the door, slamming it shut and then rushing over to her side.

Bang! Bang! Bang!

The sound of gunfire hitting the door leading to Brody's room forced her to back away from her own door.

She turned toward Brody. "Grab the table."

He seemed to read her mind, grasping one end while she took the other, moving in unison as they upended it so they could use it as a shield. Mere seconds after they dropped down behind it, a single gunman came into the room, coughing from the smoke of the extinguisher. He fired repeatedly as if he couldn't see very well.

She cringed as bullets crashed into the drywall, the bed, and from the sounds of shattering glass, she knew he'd hit the mirror over the desk.

She and Brody returned fire, and once again she heard a grunt. She guessed that one of them may have hit the gunman. The sound of pounding footsteps made her think the gunman had fled.

Brody didn't hesitate—he leaped over the table with the quickness and grace of a gazelle and rushed out after the perp. She quickly released Thunder from his leash and followed Brody, Thunder keeping pace at her side.

The smoke had already dissipated, leaving a fine white powder behind. So much for her bright idea. She found Brody standing in the center of the parking lot, watching as taillights became smaller and smaller in the distance.

"He got away." Brody's voice was hoarse, either from anger and frustration or because of the remnants of powder floating in the breeze.

"At least we're safe," she said, reaching out to grasp his arm.

"Yeah." He covered her hand with his, the expression on his ruggedly handsome face looking as if it was carved in granite. "Let's get out of here."

As much as she wanted nothing more than to get as far away from this place as possible, she shook her head. "We have to call for backup, although I'm sure by now anyone who heard the gunfire has already notified the authorities."

"Fine." Brody's tone was flat and hard. He quickly made the call and told the occupants milling about outside to stay back, out of the way. When they huddled over by the lobby, he turned to her. "It's clear this guy is after us. Getting away from here will keep everyone else safe"

By now it was more like the third attempt on their lives, but who was counting? Julianne decided it was useless to argue, especially since she didn't really want to stick around, either. *"Them?"* she asked, as they grabbed Thunder's dishes and hurried over to where they'd left Brody's SUV.

"There was a man sitting behind the wheel," Brody said. "Floored it the second the gunman climbed inside the passenger seat."

Nate, she thought, but didn't voice her theory. Instead, she looked down at Thunder who was sniffing the ground around the SUV. When he alerted near the back end, she grabbed Brody's arm.

"Don't touch it," she hissed.

To his credit, Brody instantly took a step back. "What's wrong?"

"Thunder is alerting near the back of your SUV. Remember the bomb under my FBI vehicle?"

"Yeah." Brody took another step backward and she followed. Soon they were far enough away not to be harmed by an unexpected blast. "Okay, we can't use the vehicle. But we can't leave it here…someone else might trigger the bomb."

"I know." She glanced toward the wooded area off to the east side of the building. "Let's take cover over there, we can keep an eye on both the front of the motel and the SUV while we wait for backup."

Brody must have read her mind, since he was already heading for the woods. "Rick is already on his way, but I'll request they call Eddie in as well. He's a retired cop who used to work on the bomb squad in Houston. He'll know what to do. Once the bomb has been secured, we'll have Rick take us to the sheriff's department. Isn't that where your boss left your replacement vehicle?"

She nodded, following him into the woods and taking cover behind a tree. Thunder stayed on her right while Brody hovered on the other side. The SUV was well within view of their hiding spot.

For a long moment neither of them spoke. She found herself concentrating on the familiar sound of crickets and the low belch of bullfrogs while the adrenaline that had fueled her initial reaction abruptly faded, leaving her feeling weak and shaky.

Brody reached out and wrapped his big, muscular arm around her shoulders, pulling her close. She didn't resist, holding onto him as her knees threatened to give way.

She was strong and had been in difficult spots before, but having Brody's life in jeopardy had a huge impact on her psyche, something she hadn't fully appreciated until now. Despite all the hurt they'd caused each other, he still meant so much to her and she drew strength in having him near.

"Brody." She whispered his name in the darkness and he folded her close, ducked his head and kissed her.

Brody knew his timing was awful, but he couldn't resist. Julianne had been great back there, fighting alongside him without hesitation, but the thought of anything happening to her filled him with horror and dread.

He'd do anything to keep her safe from harm.

When Julianne kissed him back, wrapping her arms around his neck, the years fell away as if they'd never been apart. He'd loved her so much. And at the moment, those old feelings resurged, slamming into him with a tsunami force.

Why hadn't he gone along with her theory about Nate possibly being responsible for Lilly's disappearance? Why had he felt the need to prove her wrong?

Why in the world had he let her go?

She finally broke off from the kiss, and buried her head against his chest. He could feel Thunder crowding close, as if wanting to be included in the embrace. The thought made him chuckle.

"What's so funny?" she asked softly.

"Thunder is feeling left out," he murmured, pressing a kiss to a spot beneath her ear. "I think he's looking for a group hug."

A joyous laugh escaped and he thought he'd never heard a sweeter sound.

"I've missed you," Julianne said, her tone wistful.

His heart thudded erratically. "I missed you, too."

Long moments passed as they held each other close, clinging to what they'd once shared. But it wasn't long before his phone vibrated with an incoming call.

Regretfully, he reached for the device. Julianne dropped her arms and moved away, giving him room.

He kept one arm anchored around her waist as he answered the call from Deputy Meyer. "Kenner."

"Boss? I'm pulling into the Thoroughbred Inn now, where are you?"

"In the woods. Drive around to the back, but keep away from my vehicle. We have reason to believe there may be a bomb planted in there. Eddie our retired bomb expert is also on his way."

"A bomb?" Rick's tone was incredulous. "What's going on around here?"

Nate, Brody thought grimly. Nate had created a human trafficking ring, dealing drugs and for all he knew was selling illegal guns. And the fact that he was using weapons like bombs and grenades was probably aimed at mocking Brody's time in the service.

The days of Clover County being a quiet and peaceful place to live were long gone.

"Be careful," he advised. "We'll watch for you."

"I take it our ride is here," Julianne said. And just that quickly, the past evaporated, leaving them firmly rooted in the present.

"Yeah." He didn't want to let go, but forced himself to drop his arm from her shoulders.

Less than thirty seconds later, twin headlights bounced around the corner. Meyer rolled over to the wooded area before coming to a stop.

"Let's go." Brody urged Julianne forward. She opened the door to the passenger seat and let Thunder go first before sliding in after him.

Brody climbed into the passenger seat. "We need to stay here until Eddie arrives."

Julianne craned her neck. "Those headlights are probably his now."

Brody tensed, hoping she was right. The possibility that the gunman might return filled him with dread. But when Eddie climbed out of his truck, he breathed a sigh of relief and went out to meet with the retired cop.

Eddie donned his bomb gear, looking like a dark chocolate Michelin man as he cautiously approached the SUV. Brody wanted to follow, but stayed back out of the way of Rick's headlights illuminating the vehicle. Brody found himself holding his breath as Eddie examined the space beneath the rear bumper.

"Found it," Eddie called out. "Bring me the box."

Brody pulled the steel box out from the back of Eddie's truck and carried it over. Eddie waited until Brody backed away before carefully dismantling the device, placing it inside the steel container.

Once the threat was neutralized, Brody assisted Eddie in placing the box containing the device in the truck bed. Then he crossed and returned to where Rick and Julianne were waiting. "We need to sweep the motel, make sure there aren't any casualties."

The three of them, along with Julianne's K-9 partner, walked over the crime scene. The front desk clerk and a few other patrons were still huddled together near the lobby doors, where Brody had instructed them to go.

Amazingly, no one else had been injured, although the same couldn't be said for the structure. Brody gave the clerk his name and information so the owner could contact him, before rejoining Rick and Julianne.

"Let's head back to the sheriff's department," he told Rick.

"Okay." Meyer shot him a concerned glance as they returned to the vehicle. "It looks like a war zone back there."

"The gunman is getting impatient," Brody agreed. Rick put the truck in gear and headed away from the bullet-ridden Thoroughbred Inn. "He pretty much emptied his clip."

"It's amazing you both managed to get away unharmed," Rick said with a dark frown.

"And the other motel guests, too." Brody glanced back at Julianne and Thunder. "They all stayed out of our way. Thankfully, we were able to improvise."

"The FBI academy must have some amazing training," Meyer said, using the rearview mirror to smile at Julianne. Brody had to tamp down the urge to tell his deputy to keep his eyes on the road.

"I need to check in with Max," she murmured.

Brody glanced at his watch. "It's four in the morning, you may want to wait until sunrise."

She shrugged and nodded. "You're right, it's not as if we have any additional evidence."

"I picked up one shell casing," Brody said. "But we'll need that Houston evidence team to go through the motel to get the rest of the bullet fragments and casings."

"They will," she assured him.

Meyer dropped them off in front of the sheriff's department. Julianne and Thunder immediately headed toward the shiny SUV. One, he was glad to see, that wasn't marked as belonging to the FBI.

"You want to drive?" Julianne asked, tossing him the keys she'd found under the mat.

He caught them with one hand. "Sure." He was surprised she'd offered, Julianne usually preferred to be behind the wheel, but then again, he knew this area better than she did.

"Where to?" she asked with a weary sigh.

"Food first." They went to a local fast-food chain to

get breakfast and coffee, eating everything in the car, although Julianne also made sure to provide food and water for Thunder, too. When they'd finished, her phone jangled loudly.

She answered the phone, putting it on speaker so he could hear, too. "What's up, Max?"

"We have a lead on the Dupree guard's brother. It's possible he may have been at the compound but managed to get away."

"What makes you think that?" Julianne asked.

"A fisherman on the Clover River reported suspicious activity at an isolated cabin in the woods. He noticed a guy entering the cabin, wearing a camouflage uniform that sounds exactly like the type all the other guards were wearing. Could be a fourth guard that ran off rather than fighting us. He could also be the one who shot the other guard in the head so he wouldn't talk."

"Unbelievable," she murmured.

"The witness claims the guy appeared to be injured. He was favoring his left leg and holding his arm close to his chest. The fisherman didn't go inside, but it wasn't long when three additional men dressed in dark clothes and wearing sunglasses arrived on the scene. Our caller hightailed it out of there, but is willing to take us back to where he was when this went down."

Brody tightened his grip on the steering wheel. A witness! This was the best news, yet.

Four attempts to kill them was four too many. They needed to turn this investigation around, rather than continue running from the shooter.

EIGHT

"That's a great break for us," Julianne said, her previous weariness replaced by a surge of anticipation. Was it possible these guys might lead them to Jake? "Tell me where we should meet you."

Max described the location and she glanced at Brody, who nodded as if he knew exactly where to go. "I know it," he said loud enough for Max to hear. "We should be able to be there in thirty to forty minutes."

"Make sure you bring the evidence bag with Jake's shirt," Max instructed. "Just in case."

"Of course," she responded, glad she'd remembered to grab her backpack as they'd left the motel. After disconnecting the line, she sat back in her seat, thinking about how the second cabin was located near water and wondering just how far it was from the Dupree house hidden deep in the woods.

"What's wrong?" Brody asked, breaking the silence.

She shook her head. "Nothing, I'm just putting the pieces together. It could be that this second cabin is being used as a staging area, and they use boats to escape along the river."

He nodded thoughtfully. "Possible. We'll know more if Thunder finds Jake's scent."

"Yes." Julianne glanced back at Thunder stretched out

in the caged area of the SUV. "But if they truly did leave via the river, there's no way Thunder will be able to continue tracking him. The trail will end at the water's edge."

A grim silence fell between them. The thought of losing Jake Morrow's trail for good was sobering. Especially when they'd already gotten so close. They'd even found his watch at the Dupree compound.

"Hey, what about Nate?" Julianne abruptly asked.

"What do you mean?"

"Isn't it possible that Nate and the gunman may have also escaped via the water?" She pulled Dylan's map from her pocket and found the river. It snaked through Clover County, heading east toward the Mississippi.

"Anything is possible," Brody admitted, his tone full of frustration. "But I'm hoping they're still hiding somewhere, rather than risk being seen. It's not as if the river is fail-safe. There are homes located sporadically along the riverbank."

"Yes, but if Dupree is using it as an escape route, it's likely others will, too." She stared out the window for a moment, watching the Texas scenery fly by. She appreciated Brody's intent of making good time.

"That's true." Brody tapped his finger on the steering wheel, an old habit that reminded her of their college days. The time before Lilly had disappeared.

The latter half of their senior year at college had been strained by their friend's disappearance and her suspicions of Nate Otwell. The day Brody told her he was certain Lilly had run away, was the day she knew he couldn't possibly care for her the same way she loved him. Her decision to join the FBI and Brody's refusal to join her had been the final breaking point.

Yet back in the woods behind the Thoroughbred Inn, being held in his arms had felt wonderful. Like coming home.

Was she really so foolish as to open her heart to Brody Kenner once again?

No, of course not. She hardened her resolve, reminding herself that whatever they once had was over and done, lost forever.

But that didn't stop her from lifting her fingers to her lips, remembering the thrilling intensity of his kiss.

She forced herself to push her personal feelings aside. She had a job to do. Allowing Brody to distract her wasn't part of her mission.

Her goal was to find Jake Morrow, Nathan Otwell and the mysterious gunman. Once she'd accomplished that, she'd join Max in continuing their manhunt in bringing Angus Dupree to justice.

Leaving Clover County Sheriff Brody Kenner behind.

Her heart squeezed painfully in her chest, but she did her best to ignore it. As promised, Brody pulled off to the side of the road where there was a narrow dirt road leading into the woods. Max, Opal, Zeke and Cheetah were already waiting, and there was an older skinny man with a scruffy gray beard and a green fishing hat standing beside them.

Their witness.

She quickly climbed out of the SUV and went around back to let Thunder out. She put him on leash, thinking she'd take him off when they had the cabin in sight.

"We're ready," Julianne said, as she and Thunder approached.

"Mr. Pickens, this is Special Agent Julianne Martinez and Sheriff Brody Kenner," Max introduced them to the fisherman.

"Nice ta meetcha," Mr. Pickens said with a nod. "But nobody calls me mister anything, I'm Frank. Just Frank."

"Okay, Frank, first I'd like to show you a photograph, see if you recognize this man." Max held out a photograph of Jake Morrow. Julianne noticed that Zeke swallowed hard, and looked away, as if seeing his half brother's smile was too painful.

Frank squinted at the photo for a long moment, then scratched at his beard. "I'm sorry, but he doesn't look familiar. The men were all wearing sunglasses."

Zeke scowled and blew out a heavy breath. Max simply nodded and returned the photo to his pocket. "It's okay, Frank. Now, if you wouldn't mind showing us the way to the cabin?"

"Sure thing." Frank Pickens spit a wad of chewing tobacco off to the side of the road, then hitched his baggy jeans up over his skinny hips before heading down the narrow dirt road.

Max and Zeke remained on either side of Frank, positioned to protect him as needed. The moment the cabin became visible, Max put out his hand to stop Frank.

"This is far enough, Frank," Max said in a quiet voice. "We'll take it from here, okay? Thanks again for your help."

Frank's expression turned to dismay. "But, I gotta show you where my boat was in the water," he protested.

"Go back to the vehicles and wait for us there," Max told him firmly. "We'll come find you once we've cleared the area."

The old man didn't look happy, but turned around and walked back toward the road. Julianne took off Thunder's leash, and pulled out her 9 mm. Thankfully they were wearing protective gear in case things got dicey.

Nobody spoke as they continued making their way toward the cabin. Julianne watched carefully for any signs of life, but there was nothing. Oddly, the windows weren't covered by heavy shades or drapes, and there didn't appear to be anyone moving around inside.

Of course, the occupants could be hiding, waiting to mount an ambush.

"Split up," Max whispered. He tapped Zeke and pointed to the left side of the cabin, gesturing for her and Brody to go in on the right. "Julianne, you and Brody cover us as we approach the cabin."

Julianne nodded, glancing over at Brody who also bobbed his head in agreement. Thunder followed close at her side as they veered away from the rough driveway. Through the trees, she could see the glistening of the sun reflecting off the water. Seeing the river helped to orient her to their location.

When they were in a good position to provide backup, she stopped behind the shelter of a tree, with the river behind her. Brody kept going until he was roughly thirty yards away from her, but still facing the cabin door.

Watching and waiting for Max and Zeke to make their way around the cabin was excruciating. Patience had never been her strongest trait. They finally came around the front, sneaking up to bracket the front door on either side. Max kicked it open and they entered, gun held at the ready. After what was only a few minutes but seemed like an hour, they emerged and gestured for Julianne and Brody to come join them.

They hastened over. "The place is empty," Max announced. "But we found a bloody shirt in the corner of the cabin. We need Thunder to check for Jake's scent."

"On it," Julianne said, turning quickly to head outside. She opened the bag containing Jake's shirt and offered it to Thunder, who buried his nose deep in Jake's scent.

"Find, Thunder. Find!"

Eager to please, Thunder immediately dropped his nose to the ground and went to work. Almost immediately he alerted on Jake's scent on a spot outside the cabin door. He continued inside the cabin leaving Julianne to follow. He alerted on several rooms, but his strongest reaction was when he came upon the bloody shirt.

Julianne caught Max's gaze. "Jake was here."

"Yeah," Max agreed. "But not anymore."

Zeke's face twisted with anguish. "So where is he? Where's my brother?"

Julianne shook her head, feeling helpless as Zeke railed at yet another roadblock in their mission to find Jake. Once again, the trail leading to the missing FBI agent had gone cold.

And they were fresh out of new leads.

Brody stepped away from Julianne in order to go through the cabin again, making sure they hadn't missed anything. It was clear Julianne's theory was right: this cabin must have been used as a staging area, either bringing people up the river to the Dupree compound, or the other way around. In the kitchen area of the cabin, he frowned as he noticed several scuff marks on the floor. There was even a distinct heel print, as if the man had walked through mud before coming inside.

The scuff marks weren't very clear, but the longer he peered down at them the more he was able to identify two distinct heel prints. One looked to be made by some sort of running shoe, while the other was shaped more like a cowboy boot.

He thought of the size-eleven print found on the door leading into the Paws and Claws Veterinary Clinic. But no, it couldn't be the same guy. This cabin was used by the Duprees, not linked to Nate and the gunman.

But was it possible they were working together? He didn't see how. They'd gotten to his compound later the same day as the jailbreak and Dupree had been long gone.

Besides, he suspected Nate was small-time compared to the money and power held by Dupree. If he understood correctly, the compound hidden in Clover County was just one of many hideouts owned by the mafia family.

And the more he thought about it, the more he was inclined to believe that finding the heel print didn't mean much: cowboy boots were way more popular in Texas than running shoes. Still, he wanted his deputies or, better yet, the crime scene techs from the Houston FBI office to come out to take measurements. He reached for his phone and took several close-up pictures, glancing over in surprise when Julianne came up to stand beside him. He drew in her honeysuckle scent, wishing he had the right to take her into his arms once again.

"What did you find?" she asked.

He pulled his head out of the clouds and gestured to the floor. "It looks to me like two people were fighting, see how jumbled up these prints are? And how it's easy to see several of the heel indentations? That's a classic sign of a physical tussle."

"Yeah." Julianne hunkered down to examine the floor more closely. Thunder came over to stand beside her, as if waiting for her to give a command. She idly scratched the dog behind his ears, her gaze narrowing. "Doesn't that look like the cowboy boot outside the veterinary clinic?"

He shrugged. "Y'all know that doesn't mean much around here. Hundreds of men and women, for that matter, wear them."

Their gazes clashed as they both remembered the flashy red cowboy boots he'd bought for Julianne on her birthday. Mere days before Lilly's disappearance and her subsequent accusations against Nate. Looking back, he realized it was probably the last time they'd been happy together.

"Do you still have them?" he asked.

To her credit she didn't pretend she didn't know what he was talking about. "No."

His chest squeezed painfully at the way she'd given away his gift.

He opened his mouth to ask what she'd done with them, but Max and Zeke chose that moment to interrupt.

"I'm going to get Frank, have him show us where his boat was located when he spotted these guys," Max said. "Julianne, I want you and Zeke to broaden the search of the area, see if we can find anything else that proves Jake and the Duprees have been here recently."

"Jake's shirt isn't enough?" Julianne asked with a frown.

Max shrugged. "Yes, but there could be other evidence, too. Something to help nail down the time frame. Since we didn't have a chance to talk to any of the guards, we have no idea if Jake was here yesterday, a week ago or longer."

"Got it." Julianne glanced down at Thunder. "We'll sweep the perimeter."

Max nodded, but didn't say anything more as he left the cabin.

"Are you planning to have the crime scene techs from Houston come here, too?" Brody asked.

"I'll call them," Zeke said as he pulled out his phone. Like Max, Zeke headed outside, leaving him and Julianne alone.

"I'm sorry," Brody offered. "It has to be hard not knowing where one of your team members is being held hostage."

She nodded, watching as Zeke walked out into the clearing. "He's taking it hard," she agreed. "I wonder if Max made the right move, bringing Zeke into the investigation."

"He's holding it together," Brody said with a confidence he didn't quite feel.

"Barely," Julianne shot back. "But he's here, so there's no use worrying about it now. Come, Thunder."

The dog immediately accompanied her outside. Once again she took the evidence bag with Jake's scent out. "Find, Thunder. Find!"

Brody watched the dog go to work, sniffing around the ground, alerting at one spot near the front door of the cabin, but then widening his search area as he attempted to pick up the scent. Brody could feel his muscles growing tense as the dog moved around the wooded area without alerting.

Julianne's expression didn't change, but he sensed she was growing puzzled by her partner's inability to latch onto Jake's trail.

Brody turned away to do some investigating of his own. Maybe he didn't have the same keen sense of smell that Thunder had, but he had a good eye and better instincts. He moved in a grid-like pattern the way he'd been taught by the army. He spied a bit of paper attached to a thorny bush, but it was so small and weathered he couldn't make out where it may have come from.

Still, he tucked it away before continuing his search. A few yards farther and he found another clue, a long bit of string also stuck to one of the thorny bushes.

The string was bright orange, and he thought for a moment about the prison-orange jumpsuit Nate had been wearing when he'd broken out of the prison van. Was it possible Nate had been here?

"Julianne," he called, leaving the orange string where it was. "Can you give Thunder Nate's scent to follow?"

"Why, did you find something?"

"Maybe." He decided not to point it out to her. He backed away from the prickly bush. "Just see if he can pick up Nate's trail."

"Why not?" Julianne sounded tired. "He hasn't found anything on Jake."

She took Thunder back toward the dirt road and gave him a treat. She'd done that before, Brody remembered and wondered if that was her way of signaling to the dog they were changing to a different scent.

It didn't take long for Thunder to head over to where the orange thread was located. At the base of the bush, Thunder alerted to Nate's scent.

"I can't believe it," Julianne said. "Both Jake and Nate were here? How is that possible?"

Brody was having trouble believing it himself. "I don't know, but see the orange string? It has to be from Nate's jumpsuit."

"But what does that mean?" Julianne's wide brown eyes were full of confusion. "Do you really think Nate is part of Dupree's empire? That your case and mine are inter-mingled together?"

He grimaced. "I wouldn't have thought so—the timing doesn't seem to work very well—but there's no denying that Nate has been here."

"What do you mean the timing is off?" Julianne asked. "I disagree. I think it makes it more likely that Nate was working with Dupree. Who better to help him escape?"

Brody still couldn't see it. "Nate is small-time compared to the Duprees. And I don't understand why a big crime family would bother with a guy like Nate. Especially since he has only been working his little drug-running, human trafficking operation for the past two to three years."

"I admit, the Duprees have been in business a lot longer than that, but I don't think we can ignore the possibility. Let's see if Thunder can prove he was in the cabin, too." Julianne led Thunder over to the open area in front of the cabin's door and once again provided Nate's scent. "Find, Thunder. Find!"

Thunder continued his zigzag pattern all the way to the

front door of the cabin without alerting. Brody couldn't understand it. None of this was making any sense.

He followed Julianne and Thunder inside, but when he looked questioningly at her, she shook her head.

Thunder went from room to room without alerting on Nate's scent.

"I don't get it," Julianne muttered, rubbing her temples as if her head hurt. "Nate was outside, but didn't come in here to hide?"

"Apparently so," Brody said. "I don't get it, either."

"Nothing about this case makes sense. Thunder, heel."

The dog trotted over to Julianne, sitting at her side and gazing up at her in doggy adoration. Brody could relate: he figured he probably looked at her in a similar way.

For all the good it did him.

"Julianne! Brody!" Zeke's shout caused them both to turn toward the cabin doorway. "Cheetah found something!"

"What?" Julianne and Thunder rushed outside.

Brody followed, his stomach churning when he discovered Zeke was holding up a running shoe.

"Where?" Julianne demanded breathlessly.

"Back this way. Find, Cheetah," he said, holding the shoe out for his Australian shepherd to sniff. "Find!"

Cheetah wound around trees, the rest of them following in single-file formation until the dog abruptly stopped. Zeke cautiously stepped forward, then reared back in shock.

"No!" His voice was a hoarse whisper.

Julianne peered around his shoulder, went pale and gripped Zeke's arm. Brody pushed past the two of them to see for himself.

He let out his breath in a low hiss. Half buried in the ground were the remains of a badly decomposing body.

NINE

"Don't, Zeke." Julianne tightened her grip on her colleague's arm. "It's not Jake. Think about it, this body has obviously been here awhile."

"But…" Zeke shook his head, unable to finish the thought.

"Come on, let's get back to the cabin." She tugged his arm, dragging him away from the body. She was only slightly aware of Brody being on the phone with Max, providing an update to their situation.

Zeke didn't resist, following her as if in a daze. She knew he still believed the body belonged to his older half brother, but she wasn't convinced. Still, she intended to use Thunder to prove him wrong.

"I have to find her," Zeke mumbled.

"Who?" Julianne asked, confused.

Zeke stumbled into the clearing. "Jake's girlfriend."

Julianne froze, then came around to stand in front of Zeke. "What are you talking about? To our knowledge Jake didn't have a girlfriend."

Zeke dragged a hand over his face then grimaced. "Several months ago, before Jake was kidnapped he confided in me," Zeke said in a dull voice. "He told me that he was seeing a woman and she'd gotten pregnant."

Julianne sucked in a harsh breath. "Pregnant?" she repeated, wondering if she hadn't heard him correctly. "Who is she? Is she still pregnant or did she have the baby? Is it a boy or a girl?"

Zeke held up a hand. "Jake refused to tell me her name, although he did say she had the baby, a little boy."

Jake had a son? "How long ago?"

Zeke shrugged. "I'm not sure. Jake mentioned the boy was about to celebrate his first birthday, but that was shortly before he disappeared. He didn't like to talk about it, he seemed upset."

"Upset?" Julianne frowned. "Why?"

"I have no idea," Zeke admitted. "To be honest I wasn't very happy to hear about it, myself. Jake should have known better than to put a woman in that position." Zeke's gaze darkened and he let out a heavy sigh. "Our dear old dad wasn't the best example of what a father should be."

Julianne tried to wrap her mind around this latest bit of news. "Jake must have given you some indication as to who she is or where she lives."

Zeke drew a deep breath. "He mentioned she lives in Montana, not far from headquarters. But if that's really Jake back there—I have to find her."

"Yeah, okay, I get what you're saying, but first of all, we don't even have an ID on the dead body. I don't believe it's Jake, and you can't act until we know for sure. In the meantime, you absolutely have to tell Max about Jake's son."

Zeke's head snapped up, his gaze clashing with hers. "Tell Max?" He clearly wasn't happy about that suggestion.

"If the Duprees find out Jake has a child they'll use that information against him, forcing him to talk. That's what this whole kidnapping thing is about, right? It's not about a ransom demand or anything else for monetary gain. It's about getting Jake to tell them what the FBI knows about the Duprees. Or worse, as a bargaining chip to convince us to release Reginald Dupree."

Zeke's mouth thinned. "Yeah, I can see your point. I don't think Jake would ever give up the location of his child, but we can't take any chances. I'll let Max know."

"You can trust him to keep the information confidential, Zeke," she assured him. "Max is a good boss. He won't get in your face about this."

"I know." He managed a crooked smile. "Thanks."

"Don't mention it." Julianne brushed away his gratitude. Then she frowned. "Hey, what size shoe does Jake wear?"

Zeke glanced down at his own feet, then back up at her. "Same as me, size twelve."

"The shoe Cheetah found was smaller than that." She looked around, finding the shoe where Cheetah had dropped it. Without picking it up, she turned it over with the toe of her shoe so that it was sitting flat on the ground. "Put your foot next to it."

Zeke did, the toe of his shoe extending a good inch and more beyond the running shoe. "It's not Jake's?"

Julianne shook her head. "I don't think so," she admitted slowly. "And I can't imagine it's Clark's, either. I'm not an expert, but I believe the body has been there for at least ten days, maybe longer. The ME will be able to tell us for sure."

Zeke looked hopeful. "You're right, it must be someone else. But who?"

She shook her head, battling a wave of helplessness. "I don't know, but we need to find out as soon as possible."

"The ME is on his way, along with a couple of my deputies," Brody informed them, sliding his phone into his pocket. "And there's Max and our witness now."

Julianne hadn't even noticed that Max and Frank had

been down by the riverbank and were now hurrying toward them.

"Show me," Max said in a curt tone. "Frank, you stay here."

Julianne led the way through the trees to the location of the body. The wind shifted and the smell was suddenly rancid, forcing her to breathe through her mouth.

"Unbelievable," Max said in a low tone. "Who do you think it is?"

Julianne filled him in on the shoe Cheetah found. "A better question is who it's not. I don't believe the body is Jake or Clark."

Brody joined them. "It could be someone from Nate's drug/prostitute business," he said. "Maybe someone who tried to get away."

"But finding the orange string and the fact that Thunder alerted on Nate's scent indicates he was here after the jailbreak, not before," she argued.

"Doesn't mean that someone working for him didn't dump a body here," Brody countered.

He was right, but she was frustrated to have so many holes in their theory, along with too many pieces to the puzzle that didn't fit.

"We won't know this person's identity anytime soon," Max said. "I doubt there will be usable fingerprints or any other convenient way to identify the body, which leaves dental records. And to do that, we need to have some idea who this person is. Unfortunately, we can't search and match dental records in ViCAP."

ViCAP was the acronym for Violent Criminal Apprehension Program, the FBI's largest criminal database. There was a gold mine of information in there, a myriad of details related to criminals and their patterns or *modi ope-*

randi. But unless their victim also happened to be a criminal, they were stuck investigating the old-fashioned way.

Painfully unearthing one clue at a time.

Brody couldn't get the image of the dead body out of his head. He felt certain the victim was linked to Nate Otwell's crimes, despite the fact that it could just as easily be connected to the Duprees.

"Julianne, see if Thunder can pick up Jake's scent out here," Max instructed. "I know the running shoe isn't the right size, but I'd like to be sure."

"Okay, but understand that the level of decomposition will make picking up Jake's scent more difficult," Julianne pointed out.

Max nodded. "I know, but there could be other bits of clothing scattered around as well."

Brody watched as Julianne took Thunder back toward the cabin. She re-established Jake's scent, then pointed toward the wooded area. "Find."

Thunder went to work and no one spoke, not even Frank, as the dog checked out the area. After twenty minutes, he alerted on Jake's scent down by the river, but not on anything near or around the area containing the dead body.

"Okay, then," Max said. "It appears Jake was here and was likely escorted to the river and taken away via a boat of some sort."

Brody glanced at Max. "I can have my deputies question the folks living along the river, see if they've noticed anything unusual."

Max lifted a brow. "Do you have any deputies to spare?"

Good point. "It will take some time," he acknowledged. "First we'll have to work this crime scene, see if we can prove the victim was killed here, or if this is a dump site. After that…" His voice trailed off. It would take several hours to clear the area. The questioning would have to wait until tomorrow.

"We could ask the Houston team to work this site," Julianne spoke up.

Max hesitated. "I've already called in several favors to the SAC in Houston. Not sure how many more I want to pile on," he admitted. "Especially when we don't know that this body is linked to our investigation and the Duprees. In fact, it seems more likely that it isn't."

"But we've been using them to help process the other crime scenes," she protested. "Why is this any different?"

Brody understood Max's concern. "Because of the timing. We're actively looking for Nate who disappeared two days ago. A body from over a week ago could mean anything."

When Julianne opened her mouth to argue further, Max held up his hand. "Let's wait for the ME to get here, okay? We'll decide what our next steps are once we have a better idea of the cause of death and the length of time we're looking at. There's no use continuing to speculate."

Zeke cleared his throat. "Boss? I'd like to speak to you for a moment." He glanced at Brody before adding, "In private."

"Sure." Max gave his dog Opal a hand signal, bringing the boxer to his side. Zeke and Cheetah fell in step beside him as they walked toward the river.

Brody couldn't help wondering what was up, and why whatever needed to be said couldn't be discussed in front of him.

"Don't worry, it doesn't have anything to do with Nate or the gunman," Julianne said as if reading his mind.

Brody shrugged, trying to sound casual. "Not my business." Except that it was. Not just because the Duprees had a hideout in his county, but because he'd been assisting the feds with working the case.

And truthfully? He didn't appreciate being treated as an outsider.

"Is that the ME?" Julianne asked, breaking into his thoughts.

"Yes, that's Dr. Lincoln Andrews," he said, gesturing toward the man who jumped out from behind the wheel of a battered pickup truck. "Doc Andrews runs a private practice here with his wife, and also functions as our medical examiner."

"Hey, uh, Sheriff?" Frank's voice drew his attention. "Do ya need anything more from me? Or can I head home?"

Brody glanced at Julianne who nodded. "I'm fine with him leaving," she said in response to his unspoken question. "We have his name and contact information if anything else comes up."

"You're free to go, Frank," Brody told him. "If you see anything else, or remember something, please let us know."

"Ah, sure thing." Frank bobbed his head and then strode quickly past the doc's truck and the two deputies to head toward the road.

"That was strange," Julianne said in a low voice.

Brody nodded. "Apparently Frank doesn't get along with our local doctor." He stepped forward to shake Dr. Andrews's hand. "Doc, sorry to drag you out here like this."

"Sheriff." Lincoln Andrews clasped his hand, then turned toward Julianne.

"Agent Martinez," she said, shaking his hand as she introduced herself. "One of our K-9 officers found the body."

Doc Andrews arched a brow. "Really? That's a new one."

"They're impressive," Brody added. He waited for the deputies to catch up. "Come on, I'll show you the way."

Despite being in his early sixties, the doc was still in good shape, easily following Brody's pace as he navigated through the trees to the area in question. The deputies spread out on either side of the site, beginning the tedious task of searching for clues. Doc Andrews set his bag on the ground at the base of a tree, pulled on a pair of gloves and went to work.

They spent hours at the crime scene, but eventually their persistence yielded results. Rick Meyers found the other running shoe, and Dan Hanson located part of a blue T-shirt and amazingly they could read the size imprinted on the back collar as being medium.

"Can you tell us anything about the body?" Brody asked Doc Andrews. "Even a rough age would help."

The ME let out a sigh. "Based on the bone structure and what's left of some of the skin and muscle, I'd say we're dealing with a young male, could be anywhere from thirteen to twenty years of age. I'll know more when I get what's left of this victim to the lab."

A sick feeling settled in Brody's gut at the idea that their victim was a teenager, rather than a grown man. For a moment his memory flashed back to that fateful night he'd followed Nate to the spot where he'd held five people hostage, ready to sell them to the highest bidder.

Each and every one of them had been younger than twenty-one years of age.

He stumbled backward, suddenly needing to get away from the body that was likely one of Nate's victims. Possibly from before he'd gotten arrested.

Bending over at the waist, he braced his hands on his knees, taking deep breaths in an effort to keep his breakfast in his belly.

"Brody? Are you okay?"

Julianne's voice was like a balm soothing his frayed nerves. He couldn't force words past his constricted throat, so he tried to nod.

"It's not your fault," she said softly, wrapping her arm around his back and holding onto him as if she were afraid he'd tumble over. "You don't know for sure this victim is linked to Nate's crimes. His death could easily be the result of two kids fighting over the same girl, drugs, anything."

After two more deep breaths, he forced himself upright. "You're wrong," he rasped. "I'm certain this kid is Nate's victim. He preyed on kids from broken families, kids that wouldn't be reported missing, or if they were, no one would think twice about the fact that they'd taken off on their own to find someplace better."

Like Lilly Ramos, he thought dully. Although he still didn't believe Lilly was dead, there was no denying that she fit the profile—her father had a heavy hand when he was drinking but her mother always bailed him out of trouble. But Lilly's parents had been convinced she had taken off on her own, searching for a job in Houston. They'd even shown computer searches that backed up their story.

Brody still believed Lilly ran away on her own. He and Nate had spent hours looking for her, checking with bus stops, taxi drivers, anyone who may have seen her. Nate had wanted to keep searching but as the weeks turned into months, even Brody was forced to admit the trail had gone cold.

This young man was different. He must have disappeared more recently, and to Brody's knowledge there hadn't been any reports of runaways or missing teens in the past year or so.

"Even if it is linked to Nate, it's not your fault," Julianne insisted. "He chose to go back to his life of crime."

Brody shook his head in disgust. "Logically I know you're right, but deep down, I can't help but think that I'm responsible. That if I hadn't joined the army, none of this would have happened."

She linked her arms around his waist and rested her head on his chest. "Don't do this to yourself," she cajoled. "Put your faith in God's plan."

He gathered her close, pressing his lips to her temple. She was right, he'd lost sight of his faith and it was well past time to get back on track. Closing his eyes, he sent up a prayer for courage, wisdom and strength to find Nate before anyone else was harmed. When he finished, his entire body felt lighter, as if a huge weight had been lifted off his shoulders.

"Um, hate to interrupt," Max said. "But Zeke and I are ready to head out."

Julianne lifted her head and subtly pulled from his embrace. Reluctantly, he let her go. "Is there something more that you need from me and Thunder?"

"No, we're going to grab a bite to eat and see if we can't get some information on this newest lead," Max said cryptically. "Are you both sticking around?"

"Yes," Julianne answered before Brody could say anything. "We'll touch base later."

"You don't have to stay," Brody told her. "This is my mess to worry about, not yours."

A flicker of hurt darkened her eyes, but then it was gone. "We're working together as a team, at least until we find Nate or the gunman. Unless you don't trust me?"

He was shocked by her statement. "Of course I trust you. Why wouldn't I?"

"Boss?" Rick Meyers interrupted them by bringing over something in a plastic evidence bag. "Look."

He eyed the item in the bag. "A key chain? Where did you find it?"

"Front pocket of the vic's jeans. Doc Andrews has the body completely uncovered now, we're just waiting for a gurney to cart him out of here."

Brody took the bag so he could examine the key chain more closely. There was a square with an *S* etched on the face and a small chain attached to a key ring. There were only two keys, one bulky key looking to belong to a car or a truck. "Did either you or Hanson recognize it?"

"Not me." Rick glanced over his shoulder at his fellow deputy who was approaching more slowly. "Dan, does this keychain look familiar to you?"

The older deputy shrugged. "Yeah, I've seen several like it. They sell them at the Gas N Go. We could ask for the list of customers, see if anyone purchased the letter *S* key chain in the past few months."

Brody wondered if the kid had bought the key ring because he'd just gotten his first car. Nausea swished in his belly and he swallowed hard. "Do that," he said. "Let me know what you find out."

"Sure." Deputy Hanson didn't spare Julianne a second glance and Brody could tell the guy's attitude bothered her. But she didn't say anything as the deputies returned to the crime scene.

Thirty minutes later, two EMTs arrived to get what was left of the body on the gurney. They wheeled it toward their ambulance and Brody knew they'd deliver it directly to Doc Andrews's lab. When they were alone, he turned to Julianne. "Guess we need to find a new place to stay."

"Yeah." They walked down the path to the spot where they'd left their vehicle. "I have to say, it's bothering me the way the gunman keeps finding us."

"I know. It bugs me, too." Brody couldn't figure out

how Nate and the gunman had the time or the technological resources to keep tracking them. "But I have another place in mind, a motel that's located on the opposite side of the town."

Julianne's smile was weary. "As long as it's not on the same level as the Broke Spoke, it works for me."

"It's a step up," he assured her. "A place called the Sunflower Motel, and they're pet-friendly."

"Sounds good to me, even though Thunder is a trained officer, not a pet."

"I know that, Julianne, but the people running a motel might not see the distinction."

"Speaking of which, we need to replace Thunder's dog dishes, food and other equipment."

"Okay. We'll stop at the same place we used earlier."

An hour later they were settled into adjoining rooms. They'd stopped for food, but thanks to the gruesome crime scene, neither one of them was very hungry.

Brody recalled how Julianne had asked about the other kids he and Nate had hung around with at the detention center. He hadn't wanted to accuse an innocent person of a horrible crime, or waste time chasing a dead end, but that was before they'd discovered the corpse.

He forced himself to write down the names of the boys he remembered. Then he headed over to the motel's small business center to borrow the computer. It wasn't easy, but he eventually found what he was looking for, an old photo on the juvie center's website. He printed it and took it back to Julianne.

"Do any of these guys look familiar?"

She carefully studied the photograph. "Maybe this guy on the end," she finally said, tapping the picture. "The facial structure looks right, as does the scar at the corner of his mouth. We'd need age progression to be sure. What's his name?"

"Kurt Royce, he was a year younger than me and Nate." For a moment he stared at the picture. "I'd forgotten about Kurt's scar—he was cut with a knife during the first week of juvie."

"Do you know where Kurt is now?" she asked.

"No, but we may be able to find out if we head down to my office. There could be a recent mug shot of him on file."

"Let's go."

He nodded, shooting up to his feet. If Julianne was right and Royce was the gunman, it would be the biggest break so far in their case.

And his biggest personal failure for not figuring it out sooner.

TEN

Julianne glanced at Brody's stern profile as he navigated the curvy highway. She could tell he was beating himself up for not thinking of Kurt Royce's telltale scar sooner, and knew this wasn't the time to bring up her second theory.

That one of his own deputies might be working with Nate and the gunman.

Turning the sequence of events over and over in her mind, she couldn't help but think an insider was the most likely explanation. Nate and his accomplice may have gotten lucky by catching a glimpse of her small K-9 logo on her SUV parked outside Rusty's, and she could also agree they'd set the trap with the bloody towels at the Broke Spoke, but finding her and Brody at the Thoroughbred Inn? That stretched the realm of her imagination. It just didn't seem likely.

Although, to be fair, Nate and Brody had been friends for over ten years. It was entirely possible that Nate knew Brody well enough to figure out where he'd go next, staying one step ahead of him that way. Still, she knew Brody was smart enough to avoid any hiding places that his former friend might remember.

Most cops didn't believe in coincidences, leading her back to a potential inside leak.

Yet wouldn't his officers be loyal to Brody? Why turn criminal, for the money? Maybe. But just because she didn't like Deputy Dan Hanson much, with his sexist attitude toward women, didn't mean he would join forces with Otwell and the gunman.

She could drive herself crazy going around and around about this.

Deciding to keep her thoughts to herself for now, she let Thunder out of the back before following Brody inside the sheriff's department headquarters. A black-haired woman with gray strands framing her face sat at a large desk lined with four wide computer screens. Other than giving them a wave and Thunder a curious glance, she didn't say anything, obviously listening to the chatter going on through her headset as her fingers flew across the keyboard.

"That's my most senior dispatcher, Corrine Haley," Brody said as he unlocked his office. "She's been a rock during these past few days. She's been putting in extra hours so that I can use more hands in the field. I don't even want to think about what my overtime bill is going to look like. The mayor is not going to be happy if I don't have anything to show for it."

"I hear you," she agreed, knowing that budget concerns plagued every agency, even federal government agencies with highly secret missions such as their K-9 unit. "Don't worry, we'll find him."

He gave a curt nod, then dropped into the chair behind his desk, quickly booting up his computer. She stood near his shoulder, watching him work. Several keystrokes later, he'd pulled up the database and began a search for Kurt Royce.

The image that popped up on the screen made her gasp. Same narrow face framed by greasy blond hair, beady eyes and scar at the corner of his mouth. "That's him! That's the gunman."

Brody surprised her by letting out a heavy groan, rubbing his hands over his face. "I should have thought of Kurt Royce earlier."

"Hey." She put a hand on his arm. "Don't do this, Brody. You knew several kids in juvie, the gunman could have been any of them."

He pulled away from her touch, jumped up to his feet and began to pace. Thunder jerked up in surprise from where he was stretched out at her feet. She calmed him by scratching his ears. "I didn't want to believe that Nate's ties went back that far." He seemed to be talking to himself. "Why didn't I look into the juvie connection sooner?"

"Brody. *Brody!*" Her sharp tone finally got his attention and he snapped out of his funk long enough to look at her. "This isn't your fault. Regret isn't going to get us anywhere. All we can do is to work forward from here."

His tortured blue eyes clung to hers for a long moment and it was all she could do not to throw herself into his arms. Maybe he hadn't trusted her six years ago, but he did now. "Don't you think I should have known Nate was hanging out with Kurt?"

"Why would you?" she countered. "Did you ever see them hanging out together?"

That seemed to bring him up short. "No, I never did," he admitted. "I guess you're right. Nate and Kurt must have grown closer while I was in the army. It's possible that's when they decided to go into 'business' together."

Julianne held her tongue. Yes, she still believed it was possible that Nate had been a crook even back while they were still in college, but this wasn't the time to harp on the past. Especially since she didn't have any proof, other than her gut instincts.

And her inherent dislike of Nate from the first time she'd met him.

"Exactly," she said, forcing a smile. "And even better, we now have something to go on."

"Yeah, we do." Brody drew a deep breath, then dropped back into his chair and initiated a new search. "I have to believe Royce owns property here, somewhere."

Her pulse thrummed with anticipation at the possibility of a new lead. They had to find Nate, and the clock was ticking. Nate knew this area well enough to find a way past the roadblocks Brody's deputies had put into place and she could only imagine that he wouldn't risk sticking around in the area for much longer.

"Look!" Brody tapped a finger against the computer screen. "Royce owns an old ranch house set on several acres of wooded land. This could be where he and Nate are hiding."

"It's possible," she agreed. "And worth checking out, because even if they're not holed up there, we may find some other clues as to where they might be."

"It will be dark outside soon," Brody said, glancing toward the window overlooking the parking lot. "But I'd still like to get over there tonight." He opened another screen and used the internet to pull up a three-dimensional satellite view of the ranch house. "This is our destination."

"I see it." Julianne still couldn't shake the nagging worry that someone else was helping Otwell and Royce in the quest for revenge. Then again, why bother sticking around at all? If they really had a cop working with them, they could easily have gotten far away from Clover County where they had a much higher likelihood of getting caught.

"Do you want to call for backup?" she asked as Brody shut down the computer.

"No, not yet. Let's see if we find anything, first." His

expression remained grim as he stood and rounded the desk. "Let's hurry, though. It would be nice to try and get there before darkness falls."

Julianne bit down the urge to once again offer Brody some sort of physical comfort as she and Thunder led the way back outside to where they'd left her borrowed vehicle. He was taking this case against Nate extremely personally.

She hated to see him suffering for mistakes that had happened a long time ago. Mistakes that included standing up for Nate, rather than believing in her, the woman he'd claimed he loved. Her heart squeezed in her chest and it hit her, then, how much she still cared about him.

Making her realize how difficult it would be to find the strength to leave Brody for a second time.

Brody gripped the steering wheel tightly, trying to corral his deep-seated anger. He was furious with Nate Otwell and Kurt Royce.

But even more so at himself.

Why hadn't he anticipated that Nate would go back to his old ways? Why hadn't he thought about the fact that it wouldn't take much, say meeting up with an old friend like Kurt Royce, to drag him back down to a life of crime?

What if they never managed to catch up with Otwell and Royce? The thought of the two of them escaping from the law was almost too much to bear.

He glanced over at Julianne, wondering why she was being so nice to him. He didn't deserve her support.

Or her friendship.

And for sure he didn't deserve her love.

Because no matter how hard he tried to justify his actions six years ago, he should have trusted her instincts. At least where Nate was concerned. Granted he didn't believe his former friend had anything to do with Lilly's disappearance but Julianne had been right not to trust Nate. After all, Nate had certainly proven himself to be a hardcore criminal.

"Brody." Julianne placed her hand on his forearm. "Please try to trust in God's plan, okay?"

That was the second time she'd mentioned that, and he remembered how nice it felt to let go of all his self-recriminations and nagging doubt. He tried to lift his heart and his mind to pray, but for some reason, the words wouldn't come.

When they were within fifty feet of the driveway leading to Kurt's ranch house, he pulled off to the side of the road and cut the engine. "From here we go in on foot."

"Understood." Julianne pushed out of the passenger side door, then went around to the back to let Thunder out.

Brody slid the strap of his automatic rifle over his shoulder and grabbed his Glock. For a moment he second-guessed his decision not to call for backup, then he shook it off. Julianne was a trained FBI agent and Thunder was a K-9 officer, as well. Three against the two of them, but he didn't really expect to find Otwell and Royce.

They may have felt safe using the place to hide that first night, but probably wouldn't have stayed for a second and for sure not for a third night.

Still, they'd go in quietly, just in case.

Julianne was kneeling beside Thunder, encouraging him to sniff Nate's scent. "Find, Thunder," she commanded in a quiet yet firm voice. "Find."

Thunder sniffed along the ground in front of the driveway and on either side of the opening, but didn't alert. Which did not come as a surprise because if Nate and Royce had driven here, their scent wouldn't be easy to detect. But up at the house would hopefully be a different story.

He took the left side of the driveway, gesturing for Julianne to stay to the right. According to the satellite map, the driveway curved to the left, and he intended to go in first. Once they'd cleared the house, they'd search for clues.

The trees surrounding the house made it difficult to see clearly. Julianne and Thunder moved stealthily on the other side of the driveway, and the moment he rounded the bend, he froze, raking his gaze over the house.

There were no lights on indicating anyone was inside, but he wasn't going to take chances. Gesturing for Julianne to stay back, he eased forward. One step, then two, until he reached the front door.

It was locked, and he edged over to the closest window. He pressed his face against the glass and peered inside.

No one was in the living room.

He heard a footstep land with a soft thud on the wooden porch, and whirled around.

Julianne.

"I told you to stay back," he gritted out.

She gave him a *yeah, right* look and gestured to the door. "Should we break in? Thunder alerted on Nate's scent near the base of the porch."

"Not yet. I want to make sure the place is clear." He moved toward the next window and was irked when she went off in the opposite direction.

He should have known better than to expect her to follow orders. Fifteen minutes later, they met up in the back of the house.

"I didn't see any sign of life, did you?" he asked.

She shook her head. "No, but Thunder keeps alerting on Nate's scent so they must have spent a fair amount of time here."

Guilt weighed heavily on his shoulders. "Okay, I checked the windows. One is open, so I'll go in first."

"Should we wait for a search warrant?"

He hesitated, knowing she had a point. "I saw bloody dressings on the kitchen table, so we can use that as reasonable suspicion."

"It's your case," she said.

He hesitated, then quickly called the judge who'd presided over Nate's case. When he explained about Royce's home and the bloody bandages on the counter, the judge agreed to execute a warrant.

"Okay, we're all set," he told her.

She waved a hand. "You're the sheriff, lead the way."

I'm sheriff for the moment, he thought. *But not for long if I don't find Nate.*

After shimmying through the bedroom window, no easy feat, he made his way through Royce's ranch house, verifying that no one was hiding inside. He opened the back door, letting Julianne and Thunder in.

"Find, Thunder. Find," Julianne said.

Thunder went to work, moving from one room to the next, alerting nonstop until Julianne called him off.

"Thunder, heel." The foxhound came over to her side, standing at attention. Brody realized he hadn't heard the dog let loose with his musical howl in the past twenty-four hours and wondered why.

"They were here," Julianne confirmed. "Have you seen anything other than the bloody bandages?"

"Not yet, but let's get to work." Brody swept his gaze over the room. He didn't intend to leave without some sort of information.

Even if that meant staying all night.

Julianne sighed as Brody returned to the living room to begin his search. She doubted there would be much to

find, but took Thunder with her down the hall to the three
bedrooms.

They were sparsely furnished with a decor that looked
as if it belonged to another era. Either Royce had inherited
the place from his folks, or he hadn't bothered to change
anything left behind by the original owners.

She tackled the master bedroom first, searching every
square inch for—what? She had no idea. But that didn't
stop her from dropping down on all fours, checking beneath the bed and dresser for any scraps left behind.

Nothing but fuzz balls of dust, indicating no one had
bothered to clean the place over the past few months.

Thunder bumped his head into her side, as if upset at the
thought she was taking over his duties. She kissed the top
of his head, then continued her investigation into the closet.

It was full of men's clothing, including a pair of worn
cowboy boots. She picked one up, and turned to look at the
sole. Hard to say for sure, but she thought it matched the
print they'd seen outside the veterinary clinic. But that
would mean Royce came here and changed out of the boots
into a different pair of shoes.

Unless he had two identical pairs of cowboy boots?

She shrugged and set the boot aside, ignoring the tiny
pang in her heart over the way she'd ditched Brody's red
cowboy boots. Now her actions seemed petty, and Brody's
dismay over hearing she'd given them away bothered her.

Focus, she reminded herself. There was nothing more
of interest in the closet, so she finished up in the master
bedroom and wandered into the first guest bedroom.

The bed was nothing more than a bare mattress, and
there were scuff marks on the metal rails of the headboard.
For a moment her stomach knotted as she imagined someone being held here against their will. She shivered and
tried to shake off the sense of foreboding.

This wasn't the time to let her imagination run wild. Turning away from the mattress, she inspected the scuffed hardwood floor.

There were deep cracks between some of the warped boards. She crouched down, running her fingertip across the board. When she raised her hand, her fingertips were blackened with dirt. A glint of something shiny caught her eye, and she realized there was something stuck between the boards.

She rubbed the spot again, revealing more gold. "Brody?"

"Yeah?" His husky voice was faint, but she heard him coming toward her. "Did you find something?"

"Maybe. Do you have a knife?"

He dug into his pocket and pulled out a small red penknife. He opened the blade and carefully handed it to her.

"Thanks." She went to work, prying the tip of the knife around the sliver of gold. Whatever was down there must have been in there a long time. Thankfully, the wood slats were old and hadn't been taken care of, so they eventually gave way, giving her enough room to pry the object out of the floor.

"What is it?" Brody asked, hunkering down next to her.

"Some sort of charm." She doubted there would be usable prints, so she rubbed the circle of gold on her pants in an attempt to clean it off. After a few minutes, she could make out the letter R engraved in the surface.

Then she turned it over, and her stomach dropped like a rock. On the other side of the charm, the letter L was clearly visible.

L. R. Lilly Ramos.

Lilly!

Julianne clearly remembered the charm Lilly wore like a talisman around her neck. The same charm that Nate Otwell had given to Lilly on her twenty-first birthday.

In that instant, Julianne knew that her initial fears all those years ago were right. Her best friend hadn't decided to run away, leaving Clover for Houston to find a job.

Finding the charm meant that Lilly had been there. In Kurt Royce's house. Back when she and Brody were still in college. Eighteen months before Brody had left to join the army.

"Is that a piece of Lilly's necklace?" Brody asked harshly, his face twisted with agony.

She closed her eyes and nodded.

A strangled sound rose from deep in his throat, seconds before he bolted from the room.

ELEVEN

I was wrong. I was wrong. I was wrong. The words beat against his skull with the force of a jackhammer, causing him to stumble as he made his way outside. Low-hanging tree branches slapped him in the face as he rushed through the woods.

I WAS WRONG!

He clenched his hands into fists and wrestled back the urge to hit something. How could he have been so clueless?

Julianne had been right all this time. Lilly hadn't run away. There was only one explanation for her necklace to be here in Royce's house. Her disappearance was obviously the result of foul play.

Had Nate turned on his girlfriend? The woman he'd claimed to love? The woman Nate himself had tried to find after she'd disappeared?

Had Nate Otwell been working with Kurt Royce on his human trafficking scheme even back then? Before he'd graduated from college? Before Brody had gone into the army?

Nausea clawed up his throat and he tamped it back with effort, determined to face his failures head-on.

His fault. He could have saved so many innocent lives

if only he'd believed Julianne, instead of the lonely kid he'd met in juvie.

The same guy who had actually saved his life, interfering when the others had ganged up on him in an attempt to beat him up.

The man he'd once called friend.

Brody dropped to his knees, bowing his head, battling wave after wave of self-loathing.

Dear Lord, why? Why not reveal the truth about Nate before now? Why let so many years pass by? Why?

Soft, warm arms wrapped around him, Julianne's honeysuckle scent somehow managing to penetrate the depths of his despair. "Don't do this to yourself, Brody," she whispered, resting her cheek against his back. "Please don't. God is the one in control here, not us."

He shook his head helplessly. "I—it's my fault—I can't…"

"No. It's Nate's fault. No one else's. His fault and Royce's. Besides, we're onto them, Brody. They're on the run because we're hot on their heels, tracking them down. You can't give up now, not when we're so close to finding them. This is the time to lean on God's strength."

Her hands were splayed across his chest, and he found himself covering them with his own, needing something good to hold onto. She squeezed him tighter, supporting him in a way he didn't deserve.

Julianne was once the best part of his life, and now he knew what a colossal mistake he'd made in letting her go.

He tried to open himself up to the Lord, silently begging for help in finding Otwell and Royce, before any more innocent people were harmed.

Please, Lord. Please show me the way.

The nausea faded, and the tight bands around his chest

loosened. Julianne was right, this was the time they needed to lean on God the most.

"I called Max, he's on his way with Zeke."

He nodded and sucked in a deep breath. Okay, enough wallowing in things he couldn't change, there was still plenty of work to do. He turned his head, barely able to see her in the darkness. "Thanks, Julianne."

She surprised him by capturing his mouth in a tender kiss before releasing him. Thunder nudged him with his nose, and he found himself smiling at the dog's attempt to cheer him up. He stood and offered her his hand. She clung to it, not letting go.

"How long before Max and Zeke get here?" he asked, trying to focus on their next steps. "We still need to scope out the area around the house, in case there are other dwellings here that they might be using as a hideout."

"Good idea. Max and Zeke said they'd be here within fifteen minutes. Cheetah, Zeke's Australian shepherd, is also good at tracking, so we can easily split up to cover the woods."

"We should finish up our search of the house, then," he said. "There may be other clues."

She nodded, continuing to hold his hand as they went back inside. It was only once they returned to the bedroom that she let him go. "This room gives me the creeps," she muttered, heading toward the closet.

"Would you rather I stay?" he asked from the doorway.

"No, go ahead and check out the other bedroom."

The next bedroom looked exactly like the previous one, bare mattress on a metal-frame bed. Determined to find something—*anything*—that may give them more information, he meticulously examined the flooring and the dresser drawers, which were all surprisingly empty.

Weird. He expected the closet to be empty, too, but it

wasn't. The sight of rusty handcuffs and other bindings lying haphazardly on the floor made the nausea return in full force.

This was where they'd held the women, he deduced. Keeping them against their will, possibly injecting them with drugs. He swallowed past the large lump in his throat, and forced himself to turn away.

Otwell and Royce would pay for their crimes.

The sound of a vehicle approaching had him moving swiftly toward the front door, weapon ready as he peered through the window. Seeing the familiar SUV with the small K-9 logo on the back helped him relax.

Reinforcements had arrived.

Julianne and Thunder came out of the bedroom to meet him. "Find anything?" she asked.

"Cuffs and bindings in the closet."

She grimaced. "Same thing I found. I didn't disturb anything, though. We may be able to lift fingerprints or skin cells with DNA evidence from them."

He nodded and opened the door, gesturing for her to go ahead of him. "Let's hope we find something more when we search the grounds."

"Julianne, Sheriff," Max greeted them. "How did you figure out the gunman's identity?"

Julianne glanced at him, as if unsure how to respond. He stepped forward. There was no point in hiding the truth about his past. "I found an old photograph from my time at the juvenile detention center. That's where I met Nate Otwell, and thankfully, Julianne recognized one of the other kids, too. When I pulled up his mug shot, she identified him as the shooter." Brody glanced at the ranch house. "Kurt Royce owns this place, and we have reason to believe he and Otwell have been working together for years. The judge presiding over Nate Otwell's case agreed to grant a search warrant. We found bloody bandages inside, but now we'd like to spread out and search the grounds before we lose all the light."

"Okay, I'll go north. Zeke, you and Cheetah head east and Julianne should take the west," Max directed. "I don't know if we need to worry as much about the south, since that's where the highway is."

"Agreed," Brody said. "Call me if you find anything."

Zeke nodded, but didn't say anything as he moved toward the east side of the woods. He and Cheetah quickly disappeared into the brush.

Brody waited until Max and Opal had gone off to the north, straight back from the house, before following Julianne and Thunder.

Neither of them spoke as they made their way through the woods. Brody concentrated on looking for signs of a trail, or a path that Otwell and Royce may have taken, but with darkness falling, he couldn't see anything but shadows.

Just when he thought they'd have to come back to search again in the morning, Thunder let out a low bark.

"Do you see something?" he called to Julianne.

"Thunder has picked up something," she replied. "I'm taking him off leash."

Brody tightened his grip on his gun and moved closer to Julianne. The moment Thunder was loose, he took off running through the trees.

"What if it's Nate?" Brody asked.

"I don't think so... Thunder would have alerted on his scent."

Brody still didn't like it. Could be Royce was skulking around these parts somewhere, too. And either one of them wouldn't hesitate to shoot the dog.

Thunder let out a musical howl, making the hairs on

Brody's arm stand up on end. "Is that a good sound or a bad one?"

"Good. Come on." Julianne pushed through the brush in the general direction the K-9 officer had taken. Suddenly Thunder appeared at Julianne's side, then spun around to go back through the woods.

"Thunder, heel!" Julianne commanded.

The animal came back to sit beside her. She clipped the leash in place. "Find, Thunder."

The dog took the lead as both he and Julianne scrambled to keep up. After about thirty feet, Brody could make out the shadow of a person tied to the base of the tree.

His heart hammering in his chest, he cautiously approached. The man looked up, the whites of his eyes clearly visible through the darkness. There was a gag tied around his head, effectively preventing the prisoner from calling for help.

He flashed the light of his phone so he could see. The man shied away, ducking his head, as if the brightness was painful.

But Brody had seen enough to recognize him. "Clark!"

"You found him?" Julianne asked, going over to work on removing the gag.

"Yes." Brody used his knife to slit through the bindings around Clark's wrists and ankles. When the gag dropped free, Clark tried to speak, his voice little more than a rough croak.

"Thank you," he managed.

Brody nodded, relieved they'd found Clark Davenport alive. At least one innocent life had been spared. Brody lifted his face to the sky, silently thanking God for showing them the way.

And in that moment, he promised himself he wouldn't question the good Lord's plan again.

* * *

Julianne pulled out her spare water bottle and offered it to Clark. "I'm FBI Agent Julianne Martinez," she said. "Here, take a few sips of this, but don't go overboard or you might get sick. How long have you been out here?"

Clark gratefully accepted the water bottle and took a long drink before answering. "Since early this morning." He frowned. "At least I think so. It's all a blur. What day is it? How long have I been gone?"

"More than twenty-four hours, I'm afraid," Julianne said gently.

Clark rubbed at his face. "Guess it could have been a day and a half," he admitted. "I need to get home. Banjo has been locked up for too long."

"Dr. Grover is taking care of your dog," Julianne assured him.

Clark let out a sigh of relief.

"Tell us what happened," Brody encouraged in a low tone.

"Some guy with a gun ambushed me at the veterinary clinic and took me hostage. Brought me to a house, and another guy met us there. The second guy held a gun on me while I provided first aid to a bullet wound in the first guy's forearm."

Brody glanced at her, and she nodded. Clark's story matched their theory of what had transpired. "Can you describe them?" Brody pressed.

Julianne rummaged in her pack for a protein bar. Poor Clark looked as if he was starving, and she doubted Otwell or Royce had offered him anything to eat.

"The guy with the wound in his arm was roughly five-ten with long dirty blond hair and a tiny scar at the corner of his mouth. The other guy was a little taller, maybe six feet tall, but really heavy, especially around the middle. He also had a shaved head and pale green eyes."

She handed Clark the protein bar. "Here, this should help tide you over for now. Thanks for the great description." She looked at Brody, her eyebrow raised questioningly.

Brody gave her a nod. "Do you remember anything else, Clark?"

The veterinary assistant looked thoughtful. "I think the shorter guy with the scar called the bigger, bald guy, Nate. But I can't remember the other guy's name."

"It's okay," Brody assured him. "Do you think you can walk out of here, Clark? Or do you want me to carry you over my shoulder?"

"I can walk," Clark said. He leaned heavily on the tree as he rose to his feet. He stumbled when he tried to take a few steps.

"Here, lean on me," Brody offered, anchoring his arm around Clark's slim waist.

Julianne and Thunder led the way back to the clearing in front of Royce's ranch house. Clark's progress was slow, but Brody showed infinite patience with their rescued victim. When Brody had lifted his face to the sky, she'd wondered if he was thanking God for sparing Clark's life.

She hoped so. Brody deserved some good news after being faced with the brutal reality of Lilly's necklace. His gut-wrenching anguish at being wrong six years ago had cut her to the bone.

Brody hadn't deserved to be betrayed by Nate Otwell. And she was fiercely glad that Brody had been the one to finally arrest him.

Now they'd have Clark's testimony, too. The veterinary assistant would be able to testify that the two men were working together after the prison break. Not to mention the evidence they'd found when they'd executed the search warrant.

The momentum was shifting in their favor. All they had to do was to find Otwell and Royce's hideout.

Before they left town for good.

A loud crash behind her had Julianne spinning around in alarm. Clark had fallen, but Brody was already lifting the younger man up. "Come on, Clark. Hang in there, it's just a little farther, see?"

Julianne crossed back to Brody. "Give me your keys, I'll bring our vehicle up the driveway."

"Fine." Brody dug out the keys and handed them to her.

She and Thunder jogged back to where Brody had parked along the side of the road. When she drove back up to the ranch house, he was still half dragging, half carrying Clark the rest of the way out of the woods.

"Here." She opened the backseat of their SUV. "Sit here, Clark."

Brody lifted him into the seat and offered a weary smile. "Did you call Max and Zeke?"

"Doing that now," she answered, pushing the call button on her phone. "Max? We found Clark Davenport, the veterinary assistant who was taken at gunpoint by Royce. Clark is dehydrated and hungry, but otherwise fine."

"Opal and I haven't found anything, so I'll head back," Max told her. "Have you heard from Zeke?"

"Negative. I'll check in with him." She disconnected the call and found Zeke's number. The phone rang several times, then went to voice mail.

A shiver of apprehension snaked down her spine.

"What's wrong?" Brody asked, sensing her distress.

"Zeke's not answering." She stared at her phone for a long moment, then tried again. This time, Zeke's phone only rang twice before going straight to voice mail. She hit the end button, wondering what was going on. If Zeke was in trouble, wouldn't they have heard something? At least Cheetah's barking if nothing else.

"Let's go after him," Brody said.

She hesitated. "What about Clark?"

"He'll be safe inside the car. I'll have him stretch out on the backseat and lock the doors. He probably needs rest more than anything."

Every cell in her body wanted to go after Zeke, but she didn't like leaving Clark alone, either. She braced herself for an argument, and was about to ask Brody to stay behind when her phone rang.

She punched the button, relieved to see Zeke's number. "Zeke? Are you okay?"

"Fine. Sorry I didn't answer when you called. Cheetah seems to have found something, though. It's hard to tell in the dark, but I'd like you and Thunder to get over here right away."

She looked questioningly at Brody, who nodded. "Clark will be fine for a few minutes especially since Max and Opal will be here soon. Let's go."

"We're on our way," she told Zeke.

Julianne kept Thunder on leash as she headed toward the spot in the woods Zeke and Cheetah had taken.

"This looks like a path," Brody said, shining the flashlight app on his phone toward the ground. "I wonder if they found another cabin."

Julianne could see what Brody meant about a path. It wasn't so much that the ground was worn with footprints, but there was definitely a gap between the trees and brush, as if someone traveled through the area on a regular basis.

The darkness surrounding them was complete now, the quarter moon in the sky not providing much assistance.

"Is that Zeke's light?" she asked, spying a brightness off to the right side of the woods.

"Looks that way." Brody didn't move his light from the ground, for which she was grateful. There were far too many twigs and branches lying around.

Thunder whined, straining at the leash. Odd behavior for her partner.

"What is it, boy?" she asked.

Thunder's nose twitched. It wasn't as if the animal was alerting on Otwell's scent, but he was clearly acting strange.

She nibbled her lip, wondering what Zeke and Cheetah had found.

Zeke's light grew closer and soon they were within talking distance. "What is it?" she asked. "More evidence?"

"I'm not sure," Zeke admitted. He turned to face them, watching as they approached. "Cheetah found a bone."

She arched a brow. Bones in the woods weren't necessarily unusual. "Probably from an animal," she said, going over to stand beside him.

"No, it's human for sure." Zeke pointed out the bone partially imbedded in the dirt and she could see what he meant.

"It looks like a femur," she said in a hushed tone.

"Yeah, and that's not all." Zeke gestured to the ground at his feet. "Cheetah was digging here. There's another bone. It's curved, so I think it might be either a tibia or fibula."

She glanced at Brody. "We'd better call the medical examiner again," she said.

Brody nodded grimly. "Could be Otwell and Royce's dump site."

She shrugged. "Seems strange to me that they'd use Royce's property as a dump site. For all we know, this could be one of their former accomplices."

"Maybe." Brody didn't look convinced.

Zeke was still hunkered down beside Cheetah, the second bone free of dirt now. He carefully pointed to the bone nestled in the soil. "Do you have any reason to believe that Otwell and Royce have accomplices that are women?" he asked.

"No, why?" Julianne couldn't bear to look at the bone Zeke pointed to. At least this gravesite didn't smell as badly as the last one they'd found.

"I'm no expert," Zeke said slowly. "But from the size and shape of this, I'd say both of these look to be that of a young female."

A woman? Julianne's gaze clashed with Brody's and she winced at the stark regret shimmering in his eyes.

Lilly.

TWELVE

Brody couldn't tear his gaze from hers, knowing Julianne was thinking along the same lines he was.

Lilly Ramos.

The devastated sympathy in Julianne's eyes had him straightening his spine. He shoved aside the wave of remorse, reminding himself that he'd agreed not to question God's plan. He turned and forced himself to look at the white object lying in the dirt. He didn't want to believe it was part of Lilly. For one thing, the bones could belong to any young woman who'd fallen prey to Otwell and Royce's illegal activities.

Secondly, Lilly had been missing for almost seven years and just because Julianne had found her friend's charm embedded in the slats of the hardwood floor didn't mean the skeleton belonged to her, too.

But the possibility, no matter how remote, was difficult to ignore.

He listened somberly as Julianne called Max to fill her boss in on the gravesite. Glancing around, he looked for something to use as a landmark so they could find the area again. Doc Andrews was likely still dealing with their previous dead body, so excavating this area would have to wait until daylight.

"Max wants us to keep the evidence where we found

it," she told him. "He thinks we should wait until morning before continuing our search."

"I agree. We need to take care of Clark anyway," Brody said.

Julianne nodded slowly. "Okay, let's get Clark something to eat, then take his official statement. The poor guy must be exhausted."

Once again, Brody was glad they'd found the young man alive, even though he couldn't quite figure out why Otwell and Royce had let him live.

Had they taken off in a hurry, assuming the kid would die before he was found? Maybe. Or they might have planned to come back to finish him off.

No one spoke as they made their way back to the clearing in front of the ranch house. Brody went over to look inside the vehicle, relieved to see Clark still stretched out, apparently asleep.

"Maybe we should take him home," Julianne said, coming over to stand beside him.

"I'd like to make a quick stop at headquarters, first," he replied.

She looked as if she wanted to argue, but then simply nodded and went around to the back to let Thunder jump in.

The traffic on the highway was light. Brody kept a keen eye on the rearview mirror as he headed back toward headquarters. When they passed a popular fast-food joint, he glanced at Julianne. "Want me to stop?"

"Yes, please." She reached behind to gently shake Clark awake. "Hey, Clark, are you hungry?"

The young man's eyes cracked open a sliver, and he nodded. "Cheeseburger," he whispered.

"Got it." Julianne settled back in her seat. "We may as well get something to eat, too. I'll feed Thunder when we get to your office."

Fifteen minutes later, the enticing aroma of burgers and fries filled the interior of the SUV. Brody pulled off in a corner of the parking lot so they could eat. Clark rubbed his face and sat upright, gratefully reaching for his food. "Thanks," he said as he stuffed a french fry into his mouth.

"You're welcome." Brody ate quickly, barely tasting the food, his mind preoccupied with finding Otwell's location.

"Are you taking me home now?" Clark asked after devouring his meal in record time. "I'd like to pick up Banjo along the way if possible."

"After you give us your statement." Brody caught his gaze in the rearview mirror. "It won't take long."

"I thought I already did," Clark said, looking confused.

"It's just a formality. I'll write it out, and we'll need you to sign it," Brody told him. When he and Julianne had finished eating, he used his radio to let the dispatch center know they were on their way.

When he pulled into the parking lot of the sheriff's department headquarters, he had a strange sense of déjà vu. Of course, it was probably because they'd never made it to the Sunflower Motel.

He helped Clark from the backseat, while Julianne took care of Thunder. When they entered the building, he was surprised to see that Sandra Levee had replaced Corrine as the dispatcher. How much time had passed? He'd lost track, his entire being focused on the case.

"Sheriff!" Sandra raked the headphones off her head, looking at him in alarm. "Is everything okay?"

"Everything's fine. We'll be in my office if I'm needed."

Sandra eyed Julianne and Thunder with curiosity, but then replaced her headphones and went back to work.

"Have a seat, Clark." Brody dropped into the chair behind his desk and booted up his computer while Julianne filled Thunder's food and water dishes. "I want you to start again at the beginning, okay? What time did you leave home to return to the veterinary clinic?"

"A few minutes before nine o'clock at night. There were two patients that needed to be cared for, a tabby cat and a poodle."

"Do you know what time the gunman came in?" Brody asked as he typed.

"It was just a few minutes later... I hadn't even gotten a chance to give the animals their medication. I heard a loud noise when he kicked in the back door."

"Go on," he encouraged.

Clark went through the sequence of events. "After I gave him the medication and the dressings, I begged him to let me take care of the animals, but he refused."

"It's okay, Clark," Julianne said gently. "Dr. Grover came in and provided what they needed."

"Is that when you left the note? Before the gunman forced you to go with him?" Brody asked.

"You found my note?" Clark looked relieved. "I'm glad."

"What kind of car was he driving?" Brody asked as he resumed typing.

"A black pickup truck, with a black cover over the bed."

Brody wondered if Otwell and Royce had been sleeping in the back of the truck since they'd joined up. "You're giving us lots of good information, Clark," he told him encouragingly. "Did they take you to your house for some reason?"

Clark shook his head. "No, the man with the scar took me to a ranch house in the woods. He told me no one would hear if I tried to shout for help."

Something didn't add up. If that were truly the case, he couldn't figure out why Thunder had alerted on Nate's scent at Clark's place. "And you said the bald guy met you at the ranch house?"

"Yeah. Not long after we got there. That's when the guy with the scar called him Nate."

"Maybe they split up," Julianne offered. "One of them took Clark's house and the other went to the clinic."

"But that means they were looking for him, specifically," Brody countered. "And had two cars, which really doesn't make sense." He turned toward Clark. "Did you recognize the bald guy? Do you know who he is?"

Clark hesitated, then nodded. "I think I figured it out. He's Nate Otwell, right? The guy you arrested for hurting my sister, Renee."

"Yes." Brody didn't like that the puzzle pieces weren't meshing neatly together, but he moved on. "Okay, so now both men are at the ranch house. Then what happened?"

Clark described how he'd cleaned and treated Royce's wound and told him how much of the antibiotic to take. "But I wasn't completely honest about that," he admitted, ducking his head.

"What do you mean?"

"I underdosed him." Clark's cheeks grew pink. "I was hoping the infection would start to spread, forcing them to go to a hospital."

Brody couldn't blame the kid for fighting the only way he knew how. "Good job. Anything else?"

"No. When I finished dressing his wound, they re-strained my arms and gagged me. Then they hauled me into the woods and tied me to the tree."

Brody finished Clark's statement and printed it out. "Take a moment to review this for accuracy before you sign it."

Clark laboriously reviewed the statement then picked up the pen and signed it. "Now can I get my dog and go home?"

"Sure." Brody set the statement aside. "Julianne, are you and Thunder ready to go?"

"Of course." She gathered up Thunder's dishes and carried them back through the main office area.

Brody stopped at Sandra's desk. "I'm driving Clark Davenport home. If anyone needs me, I'll be sticking around Clark's place, keeping an eye on things there for the rest of the night."

"I'll let the deputies know, Sheriff," Sandra said with a smile. "But wouldn't you rather have one of the other guys doing guard duty?"

"Not this time." He turned and escorted Julianne and Clark outside.

Once everyone was settled in the car, he started the engine and headed in the opposite direction of Clark's house.

"Where are you going?" Julianne asked.

He glanced over at her. "To the Sunflower Motel. Clark is going to hang around with us for the night."

"But…" Julianne's voice trailed off. "You did that on purpose."

"Yeah," Brody admitted grimly. "I don't want to believe that anyone working for me is helping Otwell and Royce, and I'm hoping this little trick will prove me wrong."

Julianne nodded. "The way we were found so quickly at the Thoroughbred Inn was suspicious."

He shouldn't have been surprised that she made the same connection he had. After all, she was smart and savvy. But he was perturbed that she hadn't mentioned her suspicions before now.

"You have a candidate in mind?" he asked.

She hesitated, then shook her head. "I've only met a couple of the deputies reporting to you. You're the one who would have the best insight into who might be swayed to do something like this."

"I'll have to think about it," he said gruffly. "I've only been sheriff for a little over three years."

Julianne glanced over her shoulder to where Clark was slumped against the window, apparently asleep. "You should start by identifying anyone that has cash flow problems. Maybe someone recently divorced or a guy who likes to gamble."

Brody nodded, thinking through the guys who reported to him. He didn't have any women on staff other than the three dispatchers. The deputies all took turns rotating through dispatch to fill in for vacations.

The inside leak, if there was one, could be any one of them, he thought with a sense of frustration.

This time, though, he wasn't going to let his personal feelings get in the way. He'd look at every single one of his men regardless of how much he liked them, in order to identify the one who may have turned on them.

The Sunflower Motel wasn't exactly inspiring, but Julianne was so exhausted she couldn't find it in her to care. She let Thunder out of the back, clipped his leash on, and took him out for a walk so he could do his business.

She was still grappling with the fact that Brody had actually set a trap for whatever deputy might be in cahoots with Nate.

The day had been one emotional roller coaster, that was for sure. She slipped her hand into her pocket, fingering the charm engraved with Lilly's initials.

Her best friend had been gone for years, but it seemed as if they may finally be able to put her to rest. If the remains Cheetah had found actually did belong to Lilly. Julianne wasn't sure if she wanted them to belong to her best friend, or not. Yet deep down, she suspected they'd found Lilly. She'd never believed the runaway story, the way Brody had.

There was no denying she had a bad feeling about the site Cheetah and Zeke had found. When you considered men like Otwell and Royce, finding one body likely meant there were more.

Many more.

With Thunder at her side, she circled the motel, checking the place out. The building was just two stories high and ten rooms along its length. She hoped Brody remembered to request rooms on the ground level.

The way he'd reacted so strongly after finding Lilly's pendant made her feel bad for him all over again. Being right about Lilly's fate didn't matter anymore.

Brody did. And she wanted, needed him to find a way to forgive himself.

The place looked innocuous enough, so she cleaned up after Thunder and met up with Brody and Clark who'd emerged from the lobby. The young man wasn't thrilled with the change in plans, but he didn't complain.

Brody handed her a key. "Clark and I are in room eight, you're in ten. They're connecting rooms in case you need anything."

"Thanks." She remembered all too clearly what had transpired at the Thoroughbred Inn. As she unlocked the door and entered her room, she frowned. Now that she thought about it, Brody hadn't reported in as to their location for that night.

So how would a deputy figure it out? Tracking via GPS? Catching a glimpse of their SUV outside the motel?

Or were they on the wrong track believing someone within law enforcement was involved?

She tried to put a halt to her whirling thoughts. They'd find out one way or another, but the possibilities plagued her as she cleaned up.

Thirty minutes later, she stretched out on top of the bed. It felt good to be clean, but so much had happened over the past few days she was finding it difficult to shut down her thoughts.

"Julianne?" Brody's soft voice came from the doorway between their rooms.

Thunder thumped his tail on the floor acknowledging Brody as a friend. She swung upright and went over to open the door wider. "Something wrong?" she whispered.

"Can't sleep." Brody glanced over his shoulder with a grimace. "And Clark snores."

For the first time in twenty-four hours, a smile tugged at the corner of her mouth. "Wow, you're not kidding." She opened the door and gestured for him to come inside.

Brody crossed over to the chair in the corner. "It's not all Clark's fault," he acknowledged. "I don't think I'd be able to sleep regardless of his snoring."

"I know. I seem to be having the same problem." She sat on the edge of the bed and dragged a hand through her hair. "Things have been crazy between our attempts to find our kidnapped agent while tracking down Otwell and Royce."

Brody's expression was thoughtful. "I feel like we're missing something. I just don't understand why they're hanging around here."

"The roadblocks you set up may have something to do with it," she pointed out.

"But that wouldn't be a problem if they really have a deputy helping them out."

"True." She'd thought the same thing. "Okay, so why else would they stick around? To find supplies? Maybe get their hands on some cash?"

Brody leaned forward propping his elbows on his knees. "Money. It's not easy to go on the run without it."

Julianne found herself staring at Brody's familiar features, wishing for something she didn't dare name. He obviously regretted believing in Nate's story about Lilly running away, but she still couldn't deny the feeling that he hadn't cared about her enough to believe in her. Was she crazy to think they could try again?

Would Brody even want to?

With an effort, she concentrated on the facts of their case. "Okay, so let's review the timeline. Royce helps Otwell escape. They're surprised to discover I've witnessed the jailbreak and Royce comes after me. But I wound him, instead, creating the first wrinkle in their plan."

Brody was nodding in agreement. "They manage to find your vehicle outside Rusty's long enough to plant a bomb. Only Thunder saves us and gets a piece of Royce's clothing. Later that night, they break into the veterinary clinic, stumbling across Clark who poses another problem for them to deal with. But they use him to their advantage, kidnapping him and forcing him to render first aid. When he's finished, they tie him to a tree and leave him to die."

"That's when they head out to the Broke Spoke, to plant the bloody towels," Julianne said. "Maybe they slept there, too. Royce's scent was all over the place, but we didn't get a chance to check other rooms for Otwell's scent."

"Two separate rooms?" Brody shrugged. "It's possible. Maybe they're not worried about spending money because they have a stash squirreled away somewhere."

"They hide somewhere nearby, using the grenade in yet another attempt to kill us," she continued. "Seems strange they wouldn't just shoot."

"We may have gotten there earlier than they expected," Brody pointed out.

She nodded. "But here is where the timing really doesn't make any sense. We have a fisherman who sees men dressed in black outside a cabin where Thunder picks up Jake's scent. We find a bit of orange string and Thunder alerts on Otwell's scent. There's a dead body, likely there at least ten days, likely longer, either related to Otwell's criminal activities or

to the Duprees'. Then we're shot at again, at the Thoroughbred Inn." She looked at Brody. "I don't know what to think."

"Me, either."

For several moments, neither of them spoke. Was it her
imagination, or were his blue eyes reflecting the same hint
of attraction she felt? She placed her hand on his arm. "I
know it's been a rough few days, but we're going to find
him, Brody."

His mouth flattened. "Too late for Lilly, or all the other
women he hurt or worse over the last ten years."

She winced at the self-recrimination in his tone. "The
crimes belong to Nate, not you."

"I wish I could believe that," he said, his voice low and
husky.

"I know you befriended Nate at the juvie center, but
that doesn't make you guilty by association. He had the
same opportunity to turn his life around that you did. He
failed. You didn't."

Brody didn't say anything for a long moment, then he
turned to look at Nate's case file, "Maybe I should review
it again, see if I can figure out where he may have stashed
some money."

She nodded, her hand slipping from his arm. She understood his need to right a perceived wrong, but she wished
he'd turn to faith, rather than beating himself up about
things that couldn't be changed.

Brody rose to his feet, the same time she did. Only a foot
of space separated them, the room shrinking around them.

"Julianne?" Hearing her name spoken in Brody's southern accent made her shiver.

"Yes?" Her voice was a breathy whisper.

He stepped closer then lifted his hands to cradle her
face. "Thanks for being such a great partner," he said before covering her mouth with his.

The hot sweetness of his kiss turned her mind to mush. She clung to his chest and lost herself in his embrace. There hadn't been anyone for her since she'd left Clover County and Brody Kenner behind.

Nobody.

She'd intentionally kept people, men mostly, at arm's length, unwilling to open herself up to the deep slashing pain of caring for someone who didn't feel the same way.

But all of that seemed ridiculous now, as she returned Brody's kiss.

Her heart still belonged to him.

When Brody lifted his head, taking ragged breaths, she rested her forehead on his chest, listening to the thump, thump, thump of his heart.

Was it possible he felt the same way?

Or was their past too much to overcome?

She lifted her head to look up at him, determined to get answers, but his phone rang. She moved away, listening as he answered it.

"Kenner," he barked.

"Sheriff? Are you all right?" Julianne could hear the concerned tone of Sandra, the dispatcher, even without the speaker being on.

Brody frowned. "Yes, why?"

"Because of the fire! I've been told that Clark Davenport's house is completely engulfed in flames."

Julianne sucked in a harsh breath as the realization sank deep into her bones.

Their trap had been sprung. Confirming her worst suspicion.

One of Brody's deputies was leaking information to Otwell.

THIRTEEN

Brody tightened his grip on the phone in disbelief. When he'd told the dispatcher he was heading to Clark's house to keep an eye on things, he hadn't expected someone would actually torch the place.

Obviously one of his deputies listened to the police scanner and betrayed him.

But who? And why? He couldn't imagine anyone, other than Nate and Royce of course, hating him this much.

"What happened," he asked hoarsely. "Do you have any idea how it started?"

"Neighbors heard a loud boom and then saw flames. We won't know anything more about what happened until the firefighters have extinguished the blaze."

"Sandra, I don't want you to say a word about talking to me, understand? I want you to tell anyone who asks that I haven't checked in yet, and that I'm not answering my cell phone."

"But Sheriff…"

"That's an order," he interrupted sharply. "Do not talk to *anyone*."

"Yeah, sure. Okay." Sandra sounded hurt by his tone, but he didn't care. He quickly disconnected the line, stared at the device in his hand, and promptly dropped it on the ground and smashed it with the heel of his boot. Then he picked up the pieces and tossed them into the trash.

The thought of anyone being able to track him, and by proximity, Julianne, made him sick to his stomach.

"Brody, I'm so sorry," Julianne said in a hushed tone.

He sighed and scrubbed the bristle along his jaw. "I should have thought of another way to prove there's an inside leak. But I never expected—" He paused, battling a wave of anger intermixed with guilt. "I'm not sure how to tell Clark his home has been destroyed."

She grasped his arm. "This isn't your fault. Whoever is working with Nate caused the damage, not you."

He shook off her hand and moved away, needing distance. Julianne was wrong, the blame for everything rested squarely on his shoulders. Starting all the way back to the night Lilly had disappeared, when he'd allowed Nate to convince him that she'd run away.

If he'd listened to Julianne all those years ago, none of this would have happened.

"You're doing it again," she said, her tone full of sadness. "I can tell you're questioning God's plan."

He ground his teeth together so hard he was surprised the enamel didn't shatter beneath the pressure. "So you're saying I shouldn't take any responsibility for my actions? I don't think that's what God had in mind."

"Of course not," was her swift response. "But what did you do, other than tell a white lie about where you were planning to spend the night? How does that make you responsible for the actions of two men desperate to kill us?"

She made it sound so easy, so simple, when it was anything but.

"Something wrong?" Clark Davenport asked, looking rumpled and fatigued in the doorway connecting their rooms. Obviously their raised voices had woken him up.

Brody braced himself as he faced the young man who'd already been through so much: his sister Renee's abuse at the hands of Nate Otwell, being kidnapped and left for dead, and now losing his home.

"Yes, Clark, I'm afraid so." Julianne crossed over to the young man. "You might want to sit down. We have some bad news…"

"Renee?" Clark asked harshly, stumbling as he headed toward a chair. "Is my sister all right?"

Brody came over to sit beside him. "Renee's fine, at least as far as I know. But I need to tell you that someone torched your house."

"My house?" Clark's eyes widened with horror, his gaze bouncing between Brody and Julianne. "Torched it? You mean it's on fire?"

"Yes." Julianne rubbed his arm, as if she could make the horror disappear. "I'm sorry, Clark. So terribly sorry to add this onto everything else you've been through."

"My dog, Banjo. You're sure Dr. Grover has him? He—wasn't in the house when the fire started, was he?"

Brody glanced at Julianne, realizing he'd never followed up with Dr. Grover to make sure his deputy had in fact dropped off Clark's dog. "We'll call her right now," he offered, then realized he'd destroyed his phone.

Julianne pulled out hers, unlocked the screen and handed it over. "She's in my contact list."

Brody listened to the ringing on the other end of the line, expecting the call to go to voice mail when a woman's sleepy voice answered. "This is Dr. Grover."

"Doc, it's Sheriff Brody Kenner. I'm sorry to bother you so late, but I have Clark Davenport here and he's worried about Banjo."

"You found Clark?" The fatigue in Dr. Grover's voice instantly vanished. "He's alive?"

"Yes, he's alive and doing all right. Do you want to talk to him?"

"Please."

Brody handed Clark Julianne's phone.

"Vanessa? I'm sorry about the mess at the clinic," Clark said in a low, tortured voice. "I didn't want to give them the drugs, but they held me at gunpoint..."

"Shh, it's all right. Don't worry, I don't care about that. I'm just glad you're safe." Brody was close enough he could just barely hear Dr. Grover's voice on the other end of the line.

"Do you have Banjo?" Clark asked.

"Yes, Clark, I've been taking care of Banjo, but he's been missing you something fierce. I know he'll be glad to see you."

Clark's expression brightened with the news. "I'm so glad he's safe with you. Thanks for watching him for me."

"You'd do the same for me, Clark," Dr. Grover said. "Just let me know when you're ready to come to pick him up, and to return to work."

"I will. Thanks." Clark handed the phone back to Brody. "Banjo is fine. Everything else in the house can be replaced."

Brody nodded, humbled by Clark's attitude. "Thanks, Doc, go back to sleep. We'll talk more tomorrow."

"Thanks for letting me know that you found Clark," she replied.

"Doc?" Brody asked before she could end the call. "Do me a favor, okay? Don't mention that you've heard Clark has been rescued or that you've spoken to me."

"Why?" she asked.

He hesitated, not sure how much to tell her. "Please trust me on this. We're still actively investigating the break-in at your clinic, along with several other crimes. I really need you to keep silent about this."

"All right," Dr. Grover agreed. "I haven't had time to talk to anyone about the incident anyway. A few patients asked about Clark, as I've been short-handed, but I claimed he'd taken a few days off."

"Hopefully this will all be over soon and things will get back to normal," he told her. "Thanks again, Doc."

"You're welcome. I hope you catch these men soon, Sheriff."

"Me, too." He ended the call and returned the phone to Julianne.

There was an awkward silence until Clark rose to his feet. "Goodnight, Sheriff. Agent Martinez."

"Goodnight, Clark." Julianne's soft voice followed Clark into their adjoining room.

Brody moved to follow Clark when Julianne stopped him by grasping his hand. "Shouldn't we try to figure out which one of your deputies is behind this?" she asked.

Her gaze begged him to stay, but he couldn't. The memory of their heated kiss was distracting enough.

"We need to get some sleep," he said, avoiding her gaze and feeling like a louse. "We'll regroup in the morning."

"Brody..." Her fingers tightened around his, and he steeled his heart lest he be tempted to kiss her again.

"Goodnight, Julianne." He gently squeezed her hand, then let her go.

This time, she didn't try to stop him as he disappeared into the room he was sharing with Clark. He left the door ajar in case she needed something, then stretched out on the bed fully dressed.

Sleep eluded him, not because of Clark's snoring, but because he couldn't stop his mind from racing from one deputy to the next in a vain attempt to figure out which one of his men had betrayed him.

Julianne allowed Thunder to jump up on the bed beside her. She looped her arm around his neck and stroked her hand over his soft coat.

She doubted she'd be able to sleep, her senses keenly attuned to their surroundings. The way Brody had trashed his phone had stunned her, but now, looking back, she didn't think they'd been traced by the device.

If that was truly the case, the dirty cop would have known they were here at the Sunflower Motel, rather than at Clark's place. Their trap had included notifying the dispatcher of their plans, which in turn had resulted in the fire bomb, or whatever device had been used to torch Clark's place.

She wondered where Otwell and Royce were right now. Was Brody's theory right that they were looking for a secret stash of cash in order to disappear for good? And if so, where?

Sleep finally claimed her, and when Thunder shifted beside her, she woke up, blinking in the darkness. Thunder's head was up, but he didn't growl or indicate anything was wrong.

After rolling out of bed she noticed a faint glow of light coming from Brody and Clark's room. She made a quick stop in the bathroom, then padded over to see what Brody was doing.

She wasn't surprised to find him sitting on the floor near the bathroom door which had been cracked open to provide him a bit of light with which to work. He glanced up at her, then returned to his notes.

"Can't sleep?" she whispered.

He shook his head. When she stayed where she was, he

set the papers aside and came over to meet her. She stepped into her room, and closed the door so they wouldn't disturb Clark.

Catching a glimpse of his notes, she realized he'd listed several names. His deputies? Probably.

"You need to try and get some rest," she chided, dropping down on the edge of the mattress. "We can continue the investigation tomorrow."

Brody shook his head, taking a seat on the chair located across from her. "I feel like we're running out of time, Julianne. The fire at Clark's house may be their last attempt to get to us."

"Why stop now?" she asked dryly.

Brody met her gaze head-on. "Because they have reason to believe we were there and that the coast is clear."

She frowned. "I'm not sure what you're getting at."

"It occurred to me that part of the reason they want us out of the way is because they're worried that I might find where they've hidden the money."

A chill crept down her spine. Brody had spent a long time investigating Otwell's illegal activities. Had these attempts on their lives been nothing more than a diversion with a side of revenge thrown in?

"Do you have places in mind?" she asked, craning her neck to peer at the notes.

"Too many," he said on a heavy sigh. He flipped a few pages, and she realized he must have been working the entire time she'd been asleep. "I keep going back to that cabin on the river, the one where we found a bit of orange string stuck to a thorny branch. Otwell may have gone there, only to be scared off by the other men Frank had noticed."

"It's possible," she agreed. "But we checked out the cabin, there wasn't anything inside."

"We used Thunder to search for scents," Brody corrected. "Your missing FBI agent, then Nate's. We didn't search for a hiding spot where they may have stashed some money. And once we found the body, there was too much activity out there for Otwell and Royce to risk going back."

"That's true." Adrenaline hummed through her veins. "We need to head back over there at first light."

"That's just one of the places we need to search," Brody said. "I also think I need to check out the place I arrested Nate."

She didn't necessarily agree. "But if that's the location, there was no reason for them not to head over there to get the money," she argued. "I think we should check out the cabin where we found the dead body, first."

"Yeah, okay. You're probably right." He shifted through the papers again and handed her the list of names. "You asked me earlier who I thought might be involved. These were the four names I came up with."

"Deputy Dan Hanson, Deputy Rick Meyer, Deputy Aaron Green and Deputy Josh Jenkins?" She looked up at him in surprise. "I only know the first two names, and while I think Deputy Hanson is a chauvinistic jerk, I can't believe either he or Rick would stoop so low as to sell you out to Otwell."

"I didn't think so, either," Brody grimly admitted. "But those are the four officers who arrived at the scene of the jailbreak. The four officers who saw you working with me. I've been going over and over the sequence of events in my mind, and while every one of my deputies has access to a police scanner and can listen in to what's going on, only those four know what you and Thunder look like."

The chill along her spine coalesced to ice. "Okay, let's just say one of these guys might be involved. Do you have any way of narrowing it down further?"

Brody scrubbed his hands over his face, grooves etched

in his face displaying the depth of his exhaustion. "That's what's been keeping me up," he finally said. "Dan Hanson has the most experience of any deputy on the force. He's been a cop for almost twenty years. I can't imagine why he'd throw it all away, unless he just can't stand the thought of working for someone younger and less experienced. He wasn't happy when I won the election to become sheriff and I suspect he plans to run against me next year."

She ached to reach out to him, to slip her arms around his waist and to bury her face against his chest, offering comfort. For Brody's sake, and maybe for her own, too. "It's probably not as personal as that," she said, striving to stay focused. "Doesn't all criminal behavior basically come down to power and greed? Do any of these—" she gestured at the list of names "—have any outstanding debt? Any reason to look for a source of easy cash?"

"I wish I knew," he admitted roughly. "I can run a check on their financials but that may not tell the entire story. Someone like Deputy Hanson could very well be tired of watching criminals getting away with making big bucks, while we chase our tails in an effort to put them behind bars."

She couldn't deny Brody had a point. More than one cop had turned to a life of crime for that exact same reason. The attitude of *if you can't beat 'em, join 'em.*

Not that she understood the sentiment, because the very thought of going from keeping the public safe and putting the bad guys behind bars, to throwing in with them was absolutely reprehensible.

She looked up at Brody. His head was tipped back, resting against the wall, and his eyes were closed. She smiled ruefully. He didn't look comfortable, but she was loath to disturb him.

He desperately needed sleep. The neon blue digits on

the small alarm clock read 2:30 a.m. Dawn would be here soon enough.

Gently taking the notes from his hands, she set them aside then returned to stretch out beside Thunder. This time, maybe because Brody was nearby, she didn't have any trouble drifting off.

The shrill ringing of her phone caused her to bolt upright, looking around in alarm. Brody was rubbing the back of his neck, blinking sleepily.

She reached over to pick up her phone from the bedside table where she'd left it charging. Max's number flashed on the screen.

"What's up?" she asked, stifling a yawn.

"Where are you?" her captain demanded.

"Huh?" She tried to gather her scattered brain cells. Light poked around from the heavy drape over the window and she was surprised to see the small alarm clock read 7:00 a.m. She and Brody had slept much longer than she'd expected. "A place called the Sunflower Motel. Why? What's going on?"

"The sheriff's department dispatcher claims Kenner isn't answering his phone."

"Yeah, I can explain…" she started, but Max quickly interrupted.

"You can fill me in later. There's a possible lead on Nate. A woman living on the river claims she saw two men paddling along the river, one of them wearing an orange prison jumpsuit."

Julianne glanced over at Brody. "They could be heading back to the cabin where we found the dead body."

"Why would they go back there?" Max asked in confusion.

"We suspect they have money stashed nearby. And the reason we've gone off grid is because we have reason to believe that one of the deputies has been leaking information to Otwell and Royce."

Max whistled. "That explains a lot."

"I know, right? Okay, where should we meet you?" she asked, joining Brody near the doorway.

"On the road outside the cabin. Maybe Thunder can help track Nate's scent."

"We're on our way," Julianne promised. She disconnected the call and gave Thunder the hand signal to come.

This was it. The best lead they had regarding the whereabouts of Otwell and Royce.

Only this time, she and Brody were not about to let the perps slip away.

FOURTEEN

"Stay here," Brody told Clark, giving him some money. "Don't go out anywhere alone. We'll let you know when it's safe to leave."

"But…" Clark began, but Brody wasn't listening. He left the motel room to join Julianne and Thunder outside. She was already putting Thunder in the back of the SUV and within moments they were on their way.

He pushed the speed limit as much as he dared, determined to reach the designated meeting point at the cabin as soon as possible.

"Please help keep us safe in Your care," Julianne whispered as the SUV ate up the miles. He silently echoed her prayer, putting his faith and their future in God's hands.

They were closer to the cabin than Max and Zeke, and he hoped the FBI agents would hurry. He didn't want to lose track of the two men.

Not this time. Not when they were this close.

"This is it," Brody said as he slowed down and pulled off to the side of the road. "Let's go."

"We're supposed to wait for Max and Zeke," Julianne protested. She slid out of the passenger seat and went around the back to let Thunder out. He was glad to see that she had the evidence bag containing Otwell's shirt in her hand.

"That's fine, you wait here while I head in," he said, pulling his weapon from its holster. "I want to see if I can get a visual."

Julianne scowled. "No way, Brody. If you're going, then I'm coming with you as backup."

He hesitated, trying to think of something to say that would convince her to stay behind, but then again, she was a trained FBI agent. Would he attempt to convince Max or Zeke to stay back?

No.

Working with Julianne these past few days had been great, she made an amazing partner. But his feelings toward her were far more complicated than the normal cop/partner relationship. She'd had every reason to resent him for being wrong about Nate and what happened to Lilly. Instead she'd been nothing but kind and supportive.

He didn't deserve her.

But that didn't stop him from loving her. More than he thought possible.

But this wasn't the time to dwell on his personal feelings for Julianne. Nor was it the time to head out alone. He wanted, needed every possible advantage to capture Otwell and Royce. "Okay, let's go."

Julianne already had the evidence bag open, offering it to Thunder. "Find, Thunder. Find!"

The K-9 officer immediately went to work, sniffing along the ground in front of the pathway leading to the cabin. Moving softly, Brody followed Julianne and Thunder through the dense brush.

Allowing her to go first went against the grain, but he couldn't argue with Thunder's keen sense of smell. If Otwell was already at the cabin, Thunder would let them know sooner rather than later.

Giving them the edge.

Julianne and Thunder slowed their pace as the cabin came into view. Brody strode up alongside them, scanning the vicinity for signs the two men had been here.

The area surrounding the cabin was vacant and quiet. Unfortunately, Thunder didn't alert on Nate's scent and Brody's hopes of finding the escaped prisoner sank. Was it possible they'd missed their quarry? That somehow Otwell and Royce had managed to get in and out in the time it took them to arrive?

Thunder was still sniffing the ground, but then went over to stand beside Julianne, waiting for his next command. The fact that Nate hadn't been behind the cabin made sense if they were using the Clover River as access to the place.

So where were they?

There! He caught a glimpse of orange through the trees. It wasn't easy, the two men were still a good hundred yards away. "I see them," he whispered. "Just to the right of a cluster of three cottonwoods."

Julianne looked in the direction he indicated and nodded. "Looks like they're off the water and are looking for something. How do you want to do this?"

Good question. He dropped into a crouch and tugged Julianne down with him so they were protected from view. Now that he had Nate in his sights, he thought it might be best to wait for Max and Zeke to back them up.

"We have to move through the woods in order to get close while remaining hidden," he said. "The clearing in front of the cabin is too open."

"We can split up, try to surround them," she suggested.

He didn't like that idea and tightened his grip on her

arm. "I say we go to the left, circling around the back of the cabin in an attempt to head them off. Text Max and tell him to take Zeke around to the right."

She pulled out her phone and quickly tapped in his instructions.

Brody took a deep breath and rose up to his feet. He stepped carefully, taking the lead around the back side of the cabin. While the building would hide them, moving quietly was key.

When he reached the corner, he paused, signaling for Julianne to stop. For several long moments they simply listened.

A loud clanking noise startled him. What in the world? He craned his head so he could look around the cabin toward the spot where he'd last seen the flash of orange. There was no sign of it now, but when the clanging noise happened again, he realized the two men must be digging in the dirt.

Had his theory been right? Was it possible they were unearthing a secret stash of cash?

His heart thundered in his chest and he tightened his grip on his Glock. They needed to hurry in order to catch them.

"Digging?" Julianne asked.

He nodded and gestured to the large tree about ten yards away. "Ready?"

She nodded, giving Thunder some sort of hand signal. The dog instantly responded by standing up straight at her side, waiting for her next move.

There was less coverage now, and Brody couldn't shake the feeling of foreboding that dogged his heels as he moved through the grass to the coverage provided by a large tree. Nate and Royce were both armed and dangerous.

Either man was likely to shoot at the slightest provocation.

The clanging sounds stopped. Fearing the men had found what they'd come for, Brody didn't stop at the tree, but continued moving toward the direction where he'd glimpsed the flash of orange.

Julianne kept pace beside him, although she'd fanned out a bit, keeping a good five yards between them. Thunder remained glued to her side, and he found himself grateful she had her K-9 partner with her.

As Brody moved through some thick brush, he abruptly stopped. The two men were less than thirty yards away. He could easily make out Nate's large heavy frame, his bald head glistening with sweat and Royce's slender build, his dirty blond hair hanging limply around his face.

Before Brody could say a word, Nate suddenly turned and looked straight at him. Their eyes locked, and in that moment pure hatred radiated from the depths of his old friend's gaze.

"Stop, police!" Brody shouted, drawing his gun.

But Nate was a fraction of a second quicker, shooting first then diving to one side at the exact same moment that Royce jutted in the opposite direction. A bullet whizzed dangerously close past Brody's ear.

"Take Nate," Julianne shouted, already rushing through the woods in the direction Royce had gone.

He didn't need any encouragement, wanting nothing more than to drag Nate back into police custody. He needed to know the truth about Lilly's disappearance.

It wasn't difficult to track Nate through the brush: the guy moved with the finesse and stealth of an elephant. But then suddenly Nate turned and fired in Brody's direction, forcing him to seek cover.

"You'll never catch me," Nate taunted.

Brody lifted his head and took up the chase. But when he heard gunfire to his right, his heart jumped into his throat.

Julianne!

Brody stumbled, managing to catch himself before he fell face first into a large thorny bush. He turned and retraced his steps, desperate to get back to her.

There was no way of knowing how close Max and Zeke were to offer assistance.

"He's down," Julianne shouted breathlessly.

Brody didn't stop until he came up on Julianne standing with her arms out holding her weapon.

"Good job," he said, but a moment too soon. Royce suddenly lifted his weapon, aiming at Julianne.

"Watch out," he yelled, firing two shots in rapid succession at the gunman, hitting him directly in the chest. Royce dropped backward, the gun falling from his limp hand and this time, he didn't move.

"Close call," she muttered, her face pale.

Brody's throat was so tight he couldn't speak. If he hadn't turned around to back her up...

He couldn't bear to finish the thought.

"Where's Nate?" Julianne asked, as if she hadn't come within a hair's breadth of being shot.

"He took off running," he admitted grimly.

Julianne opened the evidence bag again, providing Thunder Nate's scent. "Find, Thunder. Find."

The dog took off leaping through the trees, leaving the humans to follow. When Thunder reached the spot where a large hole gaped in the ground, a shovel lying on its side, he alerted on Otwell's scent.

A spark of hope flickered in Brody's chest.

Maybe with Thunder's help, they'd get the lowlife in custody after all.

* * *

Keeping pace with her four-legged partner wasn't easy, but Julianne pushed herself, unwilling to allow Nate the chance to slip away.

Bad enough that Royce had nearly shot her.

Her phone was vibrating against her hip, but she ignored it. She didn't want to slow down long enough to take the call. No doubt it was Max checking in.

The trees abruptly gave way to a wide clearing not far from the river. She could see Nate making a beeline toward the canoe they'd left behind.

"No!" Brody bellowed, putting on a burst of speed. Nate turned to shoot, but gunfire echoed through the air from the area she'd asked Max and Zeke to take.

Nate ducked and returned fire, but the shot went wild. Brody reached him then and grabbed Nate around the neck, pulling him backward out of the canoe. Both men rolled around on the ground, fighting for the upper hand.

"Attack," she commanded Thunder, using the hand signal as added emphasis. Her partner raced over to clamp his mouth around Nate's right wrist.

"Yeow!" he shrieked, dropping the gun. Brody used that moment to plant his hands on Nate's chest to keep him pressed against the ground. Thunder let go of Nate's arm and picked up the gun, bringing it over to Julianne.

She tucked Nate's weapon into the waistband of her slacks, then held her 9 mm leveled at his head. "Don't move or I'll shoot," she said in a stern voice. "Nathan Otwell, you're under arrest for escaping from a prison vehicle, aiding in the murder of the van driver and kidnapping, for starters. Anything you say can and will be used against you in a court of law." She finished providing him the Miranda rights, but he didn't seem to care.

Nate stared at her as if recognizing her for the first time.

Then he sneered. "Well, if it isn't little Julianne Martinez. You won't shoot me."

Brody placed the barrel of his gun against Nate's temple. "Maybe not, but I will."

Nate's expression faltered and he lifted his hands up in a gesture of surrender. "Okay, okay. You got me."

Brody pressed his fist firmly into Nate's chest. "Tell me about Lilly," he rasped.

Nate's gaze narrowed for a moment, then he shook his head and looked at Brody in confusion. "I don't know what you mean. What about her?"

"You murdered her, didn't you?" Brody's furious tone had Julianne taking a step closer. "The whole time you searched for her was nothing more than a charade. You knew where she was because you'd already killed her!"

Brody was shouting now and Julianne took another step closer. "Easy, Brody," she said in a calm voice. "We'll have plenty of time to question him later."

"I don't know what you're talking about," Nate repeated, his voice turning high and whiny. "You're talking like a crazy man, Brody."

"We found her body," Brody continued as if neither Julianne nor Nate had spoken. "The DNA match is already in progress. We're going to find out the truth, Nate, so why not just tell me? Say it! Tell me you killed her. Say it!"

For several long moments the two men glared at each other. Julianne didn't look away, even though she felt Max and Zeke approaching from the right.

"Yes," Nate abruptly said, his voice coming out in a low hiss. "I killed Lilly."

Brody's head reared back as if Nate had physically slugged him in the jaw. "Why? Why would you do such a thing?"

"Because she stumbled across my little prostitution

ring," Nate retorted, taking a sick sort of enjoyment out of telling Brody the gory details. "That's how I started my empire, you know. It was just a handful of girls at first, but then my business grew and grew..."

"Not anymore. We rescued Clark," Brody said, changing the subject. "He's alive and more than willing to testify against you and Royce. Oh wait, I forgot to tell you, Royce's dead."

"You think you're so smart?" Nate sneered, his face twisting into a mask of hatred. "You don't know anything. You never did. I ran my business for years, right under your nose."

For a moment Brody's body went tense. Julianne stepped forward, pulling her handcuffs from her pocket and tossing them toward Max. "Restrain him."

Max slapped the cuffs around Nate's right hand, then nudged Brody aside. Together they flipped Nate onto his stomach so they could secure his wrists behind his back. Then the two men dragged Nate to his feet.

"Check his pockets," Brody commanded.

Max fished a wad of bills from Nate's front pocket, and Brody found a similar amount of cash in the left. "Well, well, what do we have here?" Max asked. "Guess this must have been your last stop before getting out of here, for good."

Nate's lips thinned, but he didn't say anything.

"There's a hole in the ground not far from here," Brody said, filling in the gaps of the story. "That's where we found them."

"Who shot Royce?" Max asked.

"I did," Julianne said at the same time Brody said, "Me." Max lifted a brow.

"I shot first, but he wasn't dead so Brody finished him off," Julianne clarified.

Nate snorted. "Worthless piece of trash," he muttered. "Getting shot by a woman."

Julianne ignored him. "Why did you break into Clark's place?"

"Can't you guess?" Nate looked down at his prison orange in disgust. "After Royce stumbled across him at the clinic, I figured I could get into his house to find something to wear, but the kid was too skinny, especially around the waist. I couldn't even fit into one of his shirts."

"I'm surprised you didn't plan ahead with spare clothes," Julianne tsked as they surrounded Nate and walked him back through the clearing. The dirt driveway would take them back toward the highway where they'd left their vehicles. "Stupid mistake, Nate. Guess you're not very smart after all."

Nate let out a low sound and surged toward Julianne in a vain attempt to body-slam her, but of course both Max and Brody held him in place. Thunder growled in warning, and that was enough to stop him in his tracks.

"Don't sic your dog on me," he warned, shying away from her partner.

"Behave, and I won't have to," Julianne shot back.

When they reached the road Brody nodded at the SUV. "He's my prisoner, I'll take him in," he told Max.

"I'm not arguing," Max assured him. Between the two men, they stuffed Otwell in the backseat, taking the added precaution of cuffing his ankles together before shutting the door and locking him in.

"I'm riding along," Julianne said. "I'll catch up with you guys later."

"Fine with me," Max said. He and Zeke stood back as she opened the back and urged Thunder to get inside.

"You don't have to do this," Brody said, when she slid into the passenger seat.

"Yes, I do." She was beginning to get annoyed with him. "This is my case as much as it's yours, Brody."

He hesitated. "Yeah, I guess it is," he finally agreed.

She knew he was thinking about Lilly, and the remains they'd found outside Royce's ranch house. Even if the DNA didn't come back a match, she knew that there would be other victim's bodies found. Sooner or later, they'd find Lilly and she couldn't think of anything she wanted more than to give her best friend the proper church funeral and burial she deserved. Tears pricked her eyes as she realized she'd never see Lilly's bright smile again.

Nate didn't say anything during the drive back to the sheriff's department and the small jail cells located inside. She couldn't deny a sense of satisfaction that they'd soon have Nate locked up where he belonged.

Even though they still needed to identify the dead man they'd found with the keychain engraved with the letter *S*, the case was essentially over. The rest of the details would soon fall into place.

The good guys racked up one for the win column.

They'd gotten such an early start and the morning had been so eventful so far she was surprised to note that the time was just after ten in the morning. The area around the sheriff's department headquarters was surprisingly deserted, and she realized it was Sunday.

She wished she and Brody would have had a chance to attend services together, the way they used to during college. But there would be plenty of time for that moving forward.

If Brody was interested in resurrecting their former relationship. Putting the past to rest made her think they may have a chance for a future.

She was so lost in her thoughts she didn't notice that Brody had stopped the car, looking at her questioningly.

She gave him a reassuring smile, determined not to discuss their personal life in front of Nate.

She slid out of the seat and waited for Brody to come around to meet her. Together they helped Nate from the backseat, not easily considering his cuffed ankles. "Hold on, I need to get Thunder."

Brody tightened his grip on Nate's arm as she crossed over to let Thunder out of the back. "Heel," she commanded.

As she stepped closer to Brody and Nate, a flash of movement from the side of the building caught her eye. Just to her left, she saw Deputy Rick Meyer emerge from the farthest corner of the building.

"Hey, look what we found," she said in lieu of a greeting.

But Rick didn't return her smile. Instead he leveled his gun at her. "Let Otwell go, Sheriff, or I'll kill the pretty FBI agent."

FIFTEEN

The earth undulated beneath his feet as he stared at the deputy holding a gun on Julianne. Then a deep fury rushed over him. "You?" he rasped. "You're the rat leaking information to Otwell?"

"Let him go," Meyer repeated, the barrel of his gun never wavering from the invisible bull's-eye he imagined being centered on Julianne's chest. They were dressed in tactical gear, but at this range, even a bullet taken in the vest could cause serious harm.

And Meyer may not aim for center mass. This close, he could aim for her head.

"You don't want to kill a federal agent, Rick." Julianne's voice was calm, almost serene. "Why don't you put the gun away, before someone gets hurt?"

With the SUV directly behind them, there wasn't a lot of room to maneuver. Brody hated the fact that she was closer to Meyer, estimating the deputy was roughly thirty feet away.

Close enough that it would be impossible for him to miss.

"She's right, Meyer. You shoot a fed, they'll never stop until they hunt you down. Why don't you just let her go? This is between you and me. She doesn't need to be involved." Of the four men on his short list, he'd never have believed affable Rick Meyer would be the brains behind something like this.

Rick curled his upper lip in derision, as if reading his mind. "You never gave me the credit I was due, Sheriff. Julianne stays right where she is, or I start shooting, first at the kneecaps then working my way up to her head. Oh, and that goes for the dog, too."

Julianne stiffened at the threat, and Brody knew she'd never put her K-9 partner in harm's way. If Meyer so much as twitched the barrel of the gun toward Thunder, she'd do her best to take the dirty cop out.

Placing herself in the line of fire if necessary.

Not going to happen. Granted the very last thing Brody wanted was to let Nate go, not after everything they'd been through to bring him in. But a choice between Nate and Julianne was a no-brainer. Julianne would win a million times over.

Yet he didn't trust a snake like Rick Meyer to keep his word. He firmly believed that Meyer would still shoot them, even after Nate was released.

Okay, so he needed a plan.

"Now!" Meyer sharply interjected.

"Calm down, you'll give yourself a coronary," Julianne said in a bored tone. "You have us trapped, it's not as if we're going anywhere."

Brody would have smiled if he hadn't been scared spitless at the thought of something happening to her. "I'll let him go, Meyer, but I need a minute to remove the restraints from his ankles."

Meyer's gaze dropped to Nate's feet, as if noticing the cuffs encircling his ankles for the first time. "Yeah, okay, but make it quick."

Ignoring the frown Julianne leveled at him, he dropped

down to one knee and used the key to unlock the silver shackles. From this vantage point, he had a better view of Julianne's right hand giving Thunder the signal for *stay*. Despite Meyer's demand to make it quick, he purposefully fumbled a bit with the key, trying to strategize a way for them to get out of this mess alive.

When the cuffs dropped away, several things happened at once. He tossed the bracelets to the ground toward his right side, using the momentum of his hand to swiftly reach around his hip, drawing his weapon. He aimed and fired at Meyer seconds later, Julianne gave Thunder the hand signal for *attack*.

The cacophony of Thunder's barking intermingled with the sharp retort of his weapon took Meyer by surprise. Rick returned fire, but his aim thankfully didn't come close to Julianne. Brody felt a momentary flash of pain along his right bicep. Blood ran in rivulets down his arm but he ignored it, focusing instead on the way blood seeped from the wound in Meyer's thigh.

The deputy stumbled backward, waving his arms in a vain attempt to keep his balance. But it was no use. Thunder was on him in a flash, taking him to the ground, his front paws planted firmly on his chest, his razor sharp teeth dangerously close to Rick's throat.

Meyer screamed, "Get him off me!"

"Drop your gun!" Julianne demanded, rushing forward to back up her partner. Brody wanted to go over to help, but tightened his grip on Otwell instead.

Julianne took the gun from Rick's limp hand, flinging it aside. Thunder kept his jaws close to the deputy's throat, holding him, but not puncturing the skin, clearly waiting for Julianne's next command.

"Stay, Thunder," Julianne said, slapping handcuffs over Meyer's right wrist. "Heel."

Thunder didn't move for several long seconds before he released his hold on Meyer's neck and backed off. The K-9 officer didn't go far; he was on high alert as Julianne finished restraining Rick Meyer.

"What's going on?" Deputy Dan Hanson came out of the building and raked a suspicious gaze over Julianne. "What are you doing?"

"Arresting a dirty cop," Brody gritted out in a tone that didn't invite argument. Blood continued to congeal around his wound, soaking his shirt, but he didn't dare loosen his grip on Nate.

This time, Brody was determined to make his former friend pay for his crimes. Rick Meyer, too.

Hanson stared at Meyer in shock. "What is he talking about?" he demanded. "Tell them they've made a mistake."

"There's no mistake." Julianne wrenched Meyer's other arm around his back and restrained his wrists. She leveled a steady gaze at the older and somewhat chauvinistic deputy. "He shot at Brody. Can't you see the blood running down his arm? And he threatened to kill me and my K-9 partner if we didn't let Otwell go."

Hanson's gaze swiveled toward Nate. "You've got to be kidding me."

Up until now, Nate had been oddly silent, but now he let loose with a stream of curses. "You idiot! Why didn't you just shoot her right away! You let a woman and a dog get the upper hand? You useless—"

"Shut up," Brody harshly interrupted. "Not another word, understand? This would be a good time to maintain your right to remain silent."

Nate's face flushed tomato red, but he stopped mouthing off, for which Brody was grateful.

Julianne once again recited the Miranda warning, this time for Rick's benefit.

"Let's get these dirtbags inside," Hanson said. He crossed over to give Julianne a hand with Meyer, since the deputy couldn't seem to put any weight on his left leg.

Brody's breathing finally returned to normal as they managed to get their prisoners safely inside the building. His dispatcher on duty, Sandra Levee, gaped at seeing Deputy Meyer in handcuffs. "Sheriff, what in the world?" her voice trailed off, her eyes widening in horror when she noticed the trail of blood staining the floor behind them. More so from Meyer's injury to his thigh rather than Brody's wound.

"Call for an ambulance, Sandra," he instructed the dispatcher. "Meyer's wound is going to need attention."

"So is yours," Julianne said, her brow furrowed in concern.

"Flesh wound," he said, waving a hand to dismiss his injury. "Meyer's losing blood faster than I am. I may have hit the femoral artery."

"I've got a first-aid kit," Sandra offered, pulling a large square box out from beneath the dispatcher's desk.

"Lock Otwell up, we've already read him his rights." Brody shoved Nate toward Hanson. "We'll take care of Meyer's injury until the paramedics arrive."

"Yes, sir," Hanson said without hesitation. Before he shoved Nate inside, he glanced back at Julianne. "Nice work, Agent Martinez," he said in what Brody assumed was his rather lame attempt to apologize for his previous attitude.

Julianne's smile was wry. "Thanks, Deputy. Appreciate the backup."

Hanson nodded, opened the door to the cell and pushed Nate inside.

"Do we need to notify the DA's office?" Julianne asked as she removed a roll of gauze and several thick 4X4 packs of dressings from the first-aid kit. Using the packs she made a pressure dressing over the entry wound, then began wrapping the roll around Meyer's thigh in an attempt to staunch the blood flow. Then she used the deputy's belt as a tourniquet, wrapping it tightly two inches above the entry wound.

"I'll notify the DA's office tomorrow morning. Right now, my main concern is pulling my deputies off roadblock duty, freeing two officers up to watch over Meyer at the hospital. I can't risk yet another escape attempt."

When she finished with Meyer, she washed her hands and crossed over to stand beside Brody. "Let me wrap this for you. Once the ambulance gets here to pick up Meyer, I'll drive you to the hospital."

"Soon." Brody couldn't suppress a surge of satisfaction as Hanson emerged from the jail cell and relocked the door behind him.

It was over. No more innocent lives in Clover County were in jeopardy.

Yet as relieved as he was to have both men in custody, he couldn't help thinking about the fact that Julianne's involvement in his case was over. Which meant it wouldn't be long before she'd be heading back to wherever her FBI headquarters were located.

He didn't want her to go, but couldn't for the life of him think of a good, rational reason for her to stay.

Julianne's pulse was racing as she emptied the first-aid kit to patch up Brody's wound. She was known to be cool under fire, yet now her insides felt like nothing more than a puddle of goo when faced with Brody's injury. She took several deep breaths as she shoved the top of his sleeve out of the way and wound gauze around the jagged gash marring his arm.

He could have died.

She'd faced armed crooks before, and hadn't reacted this strongly when Royce had shot at her moments after the jailbreak, but for some reason, this close call with Brody made nausea swirl in her stomach. She took several deep breaths, fighting to keep the contents of her belly to stay where they belonged.

"I hope that ambulance gets here soon," she said, wrapping the last of the gauze around his arm. He'd been right that it wasn't a life-threatening injury, but she couldn't seem to squelch the flash of protectiveness that plagued her.

She wouldn't be happy until Brody's injury was assessed and treated by a physician.

The shrill wail of sirens split the air, growing louder until she could see the flashing red lights through the window.

Finally!

The two EMTs came bursting in, making a beeline for the chair where Meyer was sitting, his face pale and drawn, his arms still cuffed behind him.

"Get these restraints off him," one of the EMTs said in a harsh tone. "We need to get his blood pressure and access to his veins for an IV."

Julianne took the handcuff key from her pocket and quickly removed the shackles. Meyer caught her off guard by shoving her and staggering to his feet in a vain attempt to get away.

"Get him," Brody shouted but he needn't have worried. Meyer's left leg buckled beneath him and he collapsed on the floor in a heap.

Julianne scrambled over and cuffed Meyer's left wrist to the chair. "Listen, this former deputy is under arrest.

When you're ready to put him on the gurney, let me know and I'll transfer the cuff from the chair to the cot's frame."

"Uh, sure. Okay." The EMT's expression was one of chagrin, as if he'd felt bad for underestimating the situation.

It didn't take long for the two EMTs to establish intravenous access and to get basic vital sign information. One of them spoke into a radio, updating the paramedic base on their status, while the other unfolded the gurney.

"Hanson, I need you to ride with Meyer to the hospital until Ramsey and Stevenson can relieve you," Brody said.

"Not a problem, Sheriff," Hanson said, surprisingly agreeable. Maybe finding out his partner was dirtier than a pile of cow manure had created a positive impact on his attitude. Hanson nodded in Julianne's direction then hopped into the back of the ambulance with the EMTs.

"Time to get you to the hospital, too," she said to Brody.

"Not until someone comes to relieve me. I'm not leaving Nate here alone."

Julianne decided now wasn't the time to point out that Nate was behind bars. She knew Brody wouldn't risk a second jailbreak.

Her phone vibrated in her pocket. Recognizing Max's number she answered. "Martinez."

"What's going on?" her boss asked. "I thought you were going to check in once you dropped Otwell off."

"We found the leak in the sheriff's department," she told him. "Deputy Rick Meyer is under arrest, but on his way to the hospital."

"What happened?"

"Exchange of gunfire. Meyer suffered a gunshot wound to his left thigh, and Brody was nicked by return fire along his right bicep, so we'll leave for the hospital as soon as additional deputies arrive to relieve us."

Max whistled under his breath. "Sounds like things went sideways, but I'm glad you're both okay."

"We managed to keep everything under control." Julianne's gaze centered on Brody, her throat thickening with pent-up emotion, then she forced herself to turn away. "Thankfully Brody, Thunder and I make a great team."

There was a long pause on the other end of the line. "Julianne, is there something more going on? Something you're not telling me?"

She bit her lip. "No, there isn't anything else going on." This wasn't the time or the place to tell Max she was considering not returning to Billings with him and Zeke.

At least, not yet. She needed to talk things over with Brody. After they put the case against Nate to rest.

"Do you want us to meet you at the hospital?" Max asked.

She glanced at her watch, surprised once again to realize it was just early afternoon. "No need, I'm sure we'll be tied up here for the rest of the day. I'll touch base with you tomorrow."

"See that you do." Max's tone was firm, as if he could read her mind through the phone connection.

"Later." As she ended the call, two uniformed deputies entered the building. They headed straight over to Brody, wearing twin expressions of such grave concern, Julianne figured the word about Meyer had already gotten around.

"Glad you found Otwell," one of them said, breaking the silence.

"Me, too," Brody said. She listened as he quickly filled his deputies in on the incident with Meyer. "We need to keep these two guys separated, understand? We don't know for sure who else might be involved."

The deputies exchanged a glance. "You think there are other dirty cops?" the shorter one asked.

"No, but we still don't have the driver of the getaway car, either. So for now, we keep a close eye on these two."

"Okay, boss."

Brody looked as if he was going to say something more, but he simply nodded and turned toward Julianne. "You're not going to rest until I get my arm looked at, are you?"

For the first time since they'd slapped a set of silver bracelets around Nate's wrists, she smiled. "That's affirmative, Sheriff."

Brody let out a heavy sigh. "Fine, let's get this over with. I have things to do, and I'm sure Max needs you to return to working on your case, too."

His abrupt words sent a stab of pain zinging straight to the center of her heart. Had she misunderstood Brody's feelings toward her? She'd thought they'd connected, especially after their last kiss, but maybe she'd imagined his reaction.

Maybe, just maybe, he'd be happy to see her go.

"Keys," she said, holding out her palm. Brody handed them over. "Come, Thunder." She walked outside, heading straight for the SUV. When she opened the back, she reached in her pocket for a doggy treat. "Thanks, partner," she whispered against Thunder's silky fur before giving him the treat.

He scarfed up the biscuit then rested his head against her chest. She closed her eyes, thanking God for keeping all of them safe, then stepped back and closed the door.

The drive to Clover County Medical Center didn't take long. The waiting room was full of patients and visitors, many of whom stared with open curiosity at Thunder since he was still wearing his K-9 vest. Julianne figured they'd be in for a long wait, and it turned out she was right. At first, the words *gunshot wound* had garnered immediate attention, but once Brody's vital signs were checked, they were told to wait.

Since they were surrounded by people, this wasn't the time to get into anything personal. They also couldn't discuss the open items on their case. Several visitors asked Julianne about Thunder, forcing her to explain several times that he was a K-9 officer.

After what seemed like forever, but was only a few hours, the nurse called Brody's name. Julianne watched him go, resisting the urge to follow. She scratched the silky spot between Thunder's ears, her thoughts whirling. Not just about what was or wasn't happening between her and Brody, but going all the way back to Lilly's disappearance a little over six years ago.

How long would it take before they'd get the DNA evidence back from the lab?

She was so lost in her tumultuous thoughts that she didn't notice Brody until he was standing directly in front of her.

"What's wrong?" he asked. "You look upset."

She rose to her feet and forced a smile. "It's nothing. How's your arm?"

"I'll live," he said with a grunt. "Told you it wasn't a big deal."

She arched an eyebrow. "Yeah, but I see they gave you antibiotics, so don't try telling me the trip here wasn't necessary."

He looked at her for a long moment. "Julianne, do you think you can stay in town for a day or two? I—was hoping we'd have some time to talk."

Her heart soared with relief. "Yeah, I can stay for a while," she agreed. "I'd like to talk to you, too."

Brody's expression turned hopeful. "Do you think Max will mind?"

"I don't know, all I can do is ask. Besides, I also need a little help on a side job."

"What kind of side job?" he asked warily.

"I need to pick out a puppy to rescue." She glanced at Thunder. "Our team made a pact to adopt a puppy at each location we go to, to be trained as a future K-9 officer."

Was it her imagination or did Brody look disappointed? She'd hoped he'd appreciated the K-9 partners they worked with, but maybe that was wishful thinking on her part. Speaking about dogs and puppies abruptly had Brody smacking himself in the forehead.

"I can't believe I totally forgot about Clark Davenport? The poor guy has been alone there for hours. We need to get over to the Sunflower Motel ASAP."

Julianne nodded, knowing he was right. She shouldn't have forgotten about Clark, either.

But as they left the hospital, she made a silent promise to find a way to share her feelings with Brody when they finally had some time alone.

Even if that meant risking another rejection.

SIXTEEN

Brody tried not to stare at Julianne's beautiful profile as she navigated the SUV toward the motel so they could meet up with Clark. When her phone rang again, he reached over with his left hand to accept the call, putting the phone on speaker.

"Julianne?" Max's voice filled the interior of the car.

"Yes, what's up?" she answered.

"I just received news that we have an ID on the dead male body Cheetah found outside the cabin where our witness identified the men wearing sunglasses."

Brody tensed. "Who is it?"

"A sixteen-year-old by the name of Billy Shack. Kid disappeared out of Arkansas several weeks ago. It's been an open missing person's case ever since."

Brody swallowed hard. "So his death is likely related to Kurt Royce and Otwell's operation. Could be that Royce continued doing business until they made their plans to escape."

"Not a bad theory," Max agreed. "Anyway, I wanted to let you know."

"What about the young woman's body?" Brody asked.

"That's going to take much longer to identify," Max responded.

Brody knew the SAC was right. He disconnected the line, this latest news whirling around in his mind. He hadn't known Billy Shack, but the teenager's death still bothered him. Physically he was exhausted, but mentally he couldn't seem to stop rehashing the recent events.

Otwell's capture.

Royce's death.

Meyer's betrayal.

Julianne's imminent departure.

The last one bothered him the most. She'd agreed to stay a few days, but that didn't mean her feelings for him had changed.

Did it?

He wanted time to talk to her alone, to reconnect without worrying about finding Otwell, or being chased by gunmen.

Yet it appeared all she wanted to do was to rescue a pup before she left him for good.

Apparently the kisses and the emotional closeness they'd shared over the past few days didn't mean as much to her as they had to him.

A band of disappointment tightened around his chest, making it difficult to breathe. There had to be a way to convince her to stay. To give them a second chance. To allow him to prove that he'd changed.

But, had he?

The bitter taste of regret made it impossible to swallow. He told himself that of course he'd changed. He'd investigated his former friend and once he'd had the proof he'd needed, arrested him.

But then the memory of Lilly's pendant flashed in front of his eyes. Admitting he'd made a mistake didn't exactly change what had happened between him and Julianne six years ago.

Telling himself that everything that had taken place was part of God's plan helped keep him grounded, but the guilt refused to leave, clinging to his back like a giant blood-sucking leech.

He couldn't shake the notion of how badly he'd failed Julianne and Lilly all those years ago.

And how Lilly must have suffered as a result.

What if Otwell had set his sights on Julianne? His stomach twisted painfully. He knew better than to play the what-if game, so he did his best to shove the tumultuous thoughts from his mind.

Julianne pulled into the parking lot of the Sunflower Motel, parking in front of the room he shared with Clark. The window was dark. She stared at it with a frown.

"I thought he'd still be up since it's not that late, but maybe it's better to call him, first." She pulled out her phone.

He nodded, but his mind was still trying to grapple with the best way to approach the topic uppermost in his mind. Julianne's feelings toward him.

Would an apology help? Certainly couldn't hurt.

"Clark?" Julianne had the phone on speaker, so he could hear their conversation. "Sheriff Kenner and I are outside the motel. We didn't want to alarm you by barging in."

"Uh, okay." Clark's voice was muffled, groggy with sleep. "Do you need me to let you in?"

Julianne glanced over. "I have a key," he said. Pain shot up his arm as he reached into his back pocket. He ignored it.

The fire smoldering in the center of his chest surrounding his heart was much worse.

Five minutes later, the three of them along with Thunder were crowded in the motel room. Brody quickly filled the veterinary assistant in on everything that had transpired.

"The danger is over?" Clark's voice was full of hope. "I can go home?"

Brody glanced helplessly at Julianne, who winced. "Your home was damaged by the fire, Clark."

Clark's face fell. "Oh yeah. I forgot I don't have a home anymore."

Brody couldn't stand it. "Listen, buddy, you can bunk at my place with me for as long as you need."

"Really?" Clark asked. "But what about Banjo?"

"Your dog is more than welcome to stay, too," he assured the veterinary assistant. "You both can live with me until the fire department has finished gathering the evidence of the fire and your insurance company has finished rebuilding."

"Thanks, Sheriff," Clark said with a relieved smile.

"Evidence!" Julianne sucked in a quick breath. "I can't believe we didn't think of this before. How much of the evidence from the clinic and other crime scenes was collected by Meyer?"

A grim feeling settled over Brody. "I'm not sure," he admitted. "The FBI team collected most of it, but Rick Meyer and Dan Hanson worked the prison break. Since Meyer was working with Hanson, he may not have risked tampering with anything out of fear his partner might notice."

"But he may have," she pressed.

"Yeah." The thought of Nate getting away with any portion of the crimes he'd committed while being on the run caused his gut to twist painfully. And what about the evidence surrounding the dead woman's body they'd uncovered? He desperately needed to know if she was actually Lilly.

He automatically reached for his phone, forgetting the fact that he'd trashed it. "I need to call Hanson, see if he can verify the evidence hasn't been tainted."

"Here." Julianne handed over her phone. He took it and quickly called the dispatcher, who connected him to his most senior deputy.

"How much damage has Meyer done to our case?" he asked in a blunt tone.

"I'm trying to analyze the impact of that myself," Hanson said. "I was the one who took most of the evidence we collected into custody, and a large portion was collected by the feds. We also sent most if not all of what we found to Quantico. But if you're asking me if Meyer had the opportunity to contaminate some of the evidence? Yeah, he did."

A spotted haze of fury momentarily blinded him. "I need you to go through the evidence logs and verify what we still have and identify anything that might be missing."

"Will do," Hanson said. "Anything else?"

He rubbed his temple. "Has Nate Otwell's lawyer showed up yet?"

"No. Haven't heard from the guy."

"Okay, call this number or the Sunflower Motel if Otwell's lawyer calls to arrange a meeting. I want to be there, to make sure everything goes smoothly," Brody said. "I'll get a replacement phone tomorrow." He paused, then added, "I need your help on this thing, Hanson. We need to make sure both Otwell and Meyer stay in our custody. No screwups."

"The word about Meyer has already gotten out," Hanson assured him. "No one likes being associated with a dirty cop. Trust me, there isn't a deputy on our staff that is willing to let either one of these guys out of sight."

The tension eased, and as he ended the call it occurred to Brody that if Hanson could check his attitude at the door, he'd make a good sheriff.

Wait a minute, what was he saying? He didn't plan on leaving his job or his home in Clover County. He had a life here. A community he cared about. Yet the thought of losing Julianne made him realize he'd leave it all at the drop of a hat.

If she asked him to.

Julianne took Thunder and slipped through the connecting door to her room. Brody had suggested they grab some sleep before checking out in the morning.

Considering he was sharing a room with Clark, she decided it would be better to talk to Brody after they'd tied up the loose ends on their case. She hoped that rescuing a puppy might convince Brody to consider partnering with a K-9 cop.

Would she ever actually leave the FBI in order to join forces with Brody here in Clover? Not an easy decision considering how much she loved her job. Besides, abandoning Max West and the rest of her team in the middle of a case wasn't happening. No way would she let them down.

But maybe once they'd found Jake Morrow and hopefully arrested the mafia second-in-command, Angus Dupree, she could give her notice.

She'd move back to Clover, Texas, if it meant being with Brody. She'd left him once before and couldn't bear the thought of doing that again.

But first they needed to talk. To see if he was as willing as she was to try again.

Despite her tumultuous thoughts, she managed to sleep. When she awoke bright rays of sunshine filled the gap between the heavy curtains.

Thunder lifted his head, then laid it back down as she rolled out of bed and padded to the bathroom. After using the facilities, she took Thunder outside to care for his needs.

The bright Texas sky radiated warmth. Living in Montana for the past couple of years, she'd forgotten how hot it was in the south. The Big Thicket region was wooded, but a good portion of the Lone Star State stretched flat for miles and miles.

She had to admit, she'd gotten used to the mountain view outside her window back home.

Enough, she told herself sternly. Talk about putting the cart before the horse. She wasn't sure how Brody felt about their rekindled relationship. Or even if they *had* a rekindled relationship.

Was it possible they could put the past to rest once and for all? She was willing to try if he was.

"Good morning." Brody's deep drawl interrupted her thoughts.

She looked up to find him standing outside the motel door, watching her and Thunder. The danger was over, but Brody's stance was protective, and the way he continued sweeping his electric-blue gaze over the area spoke of an ingrained habit for a cop on duty. "Morning," she responded.

He opened his mouth to say something, but Clark appeared behind him. "Julianne, I hear you're looking to rescue a puppy."

"Good morning, Clark. Yes, it's a bit of tradition within our team to look for puppies when we're on assignment to adopt and train them as the next generation of K-9 cops. Do you know where the closest shelter is?"

"As a matter of fact, I do. It's only a few miles past our clinic—Dr. Grover provides free medical services to the animals at the Clover County Rescue Shelter."

"Great! That sounds perfect." She smiled at Brody, but he didn't look nearly as enthusiastic. "Do you think we can stop over there yet this morning?"

"Yeah, but first I need to stop in at headquarters, to

check in on Otwell. Then we have a couple errands to run, but once that's finished, we can head over to the shelter."

"Sounds good."

The ride back to the sheriff's department didn't take long. Hanson was sleeping at his desk, and Brody gave him a nudge. "Go home, Dan. You need some shut-eye."

Hanson blinked and nodded. "Yeah, okay."

"What's the word on Meyer?" Brody asked as the deputy sluggishly rose to his feet.

"He's out of surgery. Should be released in a couple of days. I have two deputies guarding his room at all times."

"Good, thanks." Brody motioned him toward the door. "Take off, I'll see you later."

Hanson nodded and shuffled away, yawning widely.

Julianne followed Brody over to where the two jail cells were located. Otwell was safely behind bars, stretched out on the bunk, with his hands behind his head as if he didn't have a care in the world.

Julianne averted her gaze, not willing to think about what he may have done to Lilly.

"Sheriff?" Corrine Haley called out. "Mr. Otwell's lawyer just called, asking to see his client."

"That's fine. I'll stick around while he's here." Brody glanced at Julianne. "Would you be willing to take Clark to the store and then drop him off at my place?"

"Sure, but what about your replacement phone?" she asked.

"I'll have to get it later."

"Why don't you let me and Thunder stay here to watch over Nate and his lawyer?" she asked. "Would be easier all the way around."

Brody hesitated, and she could tell he wasn't thrilled with the idea. Despite telling her she made a great partner, it was clear he still didn't see her as a capable federal agent.

And in that moment, her hopes of staying here in Clover and taking over Meyer's job as a deputy shriveled up and died.

How could she work for a man who didn't believe she was an expert in her field? "Forget it," she said, abruptly turning away. "I'll give Max a call to come and pick me up. Maybe I'll see you later. Thunder, heel. Stay," she commanded, drawing her partner to her side.

"I wish I could train Banjo to be a K-9 cop," Clark said with admiration.

She smiled at the veterinary assistant. "K-9 training starts early in a dog's life, but there are plenty of basic commands you can teach Banjo."

"Julianne, wait," Brody said, halting her progress.

She glanced over her shoulder. "Yes?"

"If you'll stay here, I'll run errands. I should be able to meet you back here in an hour or so."

A flicker of hope glowed in her heart. "Are you sure?"

"Absolutely. Come on, Clark. Let's get out of here."

Julianne returned to the desk Hanson had vacated, as Corrine stared after Brody thoughtfully. "This has been a difficult week for him," Corrine said.

"I know." Julianne scratched Thunder behind the ears, realizing Corrine didn't know the half of it.

Nate's lawyer called, claiming something came up that required him to reschedule their meeting, which was fine with Julianne. True to his word, Brody returned in just under an hour. One of his deputies arrived shortly thereafter, taking over the task of watching over Nate.

"Ready to go to the shelter?" Brody asked.

"Of course." Julianne and Thunder followed him out into the hot Texas sun.

Now that they were finally alone, she tried to think of a way to broach the subject of their tenuous relationship.

"Tell me about the team's promise to rescue puppies," Brody said, breaking into her thoughts. "Do you look for pure breeds? After all, Thunder's a purebred English foxhound, isn't he?"

"Yes, but we're open to either a purebred or mix. There are plenty of studies that have shown that with the right training, even mixed-breed dogs can become great K-9 officers. Of course, not every one of them makes it—some just don't have the right temperament. But we're doing this as a way to honor our missing agent, Jake Morrow. We also need to keep working on the next generation of K-9 officers."

Brody nodded thoughtfully. He turned the SUV into the parking lot of a large building boasting the sign Clover County Rescue Shelter.

She put Thunder on leash and took him along inside. The owner greeted them with a broad smile.

"I'm Angie Patton. Dr. Grover told me to expect you," she said, shaking their hands. "Oh, and what a beautiful dog!"

"Thunder, heel," Julianne said and her partner instantly dropped his hindquarters onto the floor, sitting straight and tall.

"Impressive," Angie said in awe. "I haven't worked with many well-trained dogs."

"Thank you," Julianne said. "I'm looking for a puppy to train as a possible K-9 officer. Will you show me what you have?"

"Certainly, right this way." Angie led them down a hallway of metal cages holding a variety of animals, most of them older than what she was looking for, yet heartbreaking just the same.

"I'm not sure how you work here without taking every one of these animals home with you," Julianne said softly.

Angie's smile was sad. "It's hard, but we're pretty good at finding homes for our rescues. Here are the two young pups I just received a few days ago."

"Oh." Julianne drew in an excited breath at the sight of the two rather mangy-looking puppies cuddled together in the corner of the cage. "They're adorable!"

"They look a little pathetic to me," Brody said, his gruff tone full of uncertainty. "Do you have any idea what breed they are?"

Angie shrugged. "They're brothers and according to Dr. Grover, they're mostly German shepherd, with a little boxer thrown in. We call the gray/tan one Cooper and the brown-and-black one Hawk."

"Can I see them?" Julianne asked.

"Of course. I guess I don't have to worry about your dog acting out," she said, opening the door.

The two pups managed to disentangle themselves from each other long enough to scamper over to greet her. They both instantly crawled up onto her lap, their little tongues attempting to lick her face.

"They are so precious," she cooed, looking from one to the other. Cooper and Hawk were wiggling with joy as she stroked their baby-soft fur. She noticed Thunder was still sitting in place, but he was craning his neck toward the pups, his nose drawn to their scent. "Thunder, come."

Her partner didn't need to be asked twice. He instantly came over, sniffing each dog, his tail wagging in greeting. Cooper and Hawk let out high-pitched yips of excitement, crawling over her in order to get closer to Thunder.

Cooper was so excited he slid from her lap, tumbling onto the concrete floor. Brody quickly bent down to scoop the little guy into his hands.

"Hey, are you okay, little buddy?" he asked.

Julianne's heart melted as she watched Brody with Cooper. "You're good with dogs," she said with warm approval. "Have you thought about a K-9 partner?"

Brody's blue eyes met hers. "Yes, now that I've had an opportunity to work with you and Thunder. You've made me realize how much I've missed over the past few years, Julianne." He hesitated, then continued, "I know it's mostly my own fault, but I'd like a second chance. With you."

Her heart soared with hope. "Not all your fault," she corrected. "I should have been more patient. And I'd like the chance to move forward from here, too."

Cooper chose that moment to slather doggie kisses all over Brody's face, making him laugh.

Hawk whimpered at being separated from his brother and the thought of splitting these guys up was too much to bear.

"How about we adopt both of them?" Brody suggested.

The flicker of hope blossomed into a roaring campfire. "I'd like that, too," she managed.

Still cradling the pup against his chest, Brody knelt beside her. "I'd like to apologize, for not believing in you all those years ago."

Tears burned her eyes, and she attempted to blink them back. "I told you, Brody, there's no need to apologize. I've been telling you all along, this is part of God's plan."

"I'm trying to believe that," he said, his blue eyes boring into hers. "Letting go of the guilt isn't easy, but I'll keep trying."

She smiled. "And I'll keep praying. For us."

"Thank you." Brody leaned forward and crushed her mouth with a quick, hard kiss. Cooper and Hawk began yipping again, climbing over each other to lick them in the face.

Dazed from Brody's mind-numbing kiss, she looked up at Angie. "We'd like to adopt these two pups, please."

Angie nodded, then went into the usual spiel about the documentation they'd need and the required neutering, but Julianne wasn't listening.

Max wouldn't be happy, but she knew that she and Brody deserved this time together.

And more.

SEVENTEEN

"Hey, Max, what's up?" Julianne asked, shifting the puppy to her other arm as she listened to Max. She grimaced and looked at Brody as she answered, "Yes, of course. We'll meet you there." She ended the call. "We need to head over to the motel to meet Max and Zeke. Results from the lab in Quantico are starting to come in."

Brody hated leaving Cooper and Hawk behind, but he understood that Julianne had little choice but to respond to her boss's summons. "No problem." He held Cooper a moment longer, then placed the pup back in the kennel with his brother, Hawk. Angie latched the cage door.

Thunder let out his oddly musical howl as they left the shelter. Brody glanced at the K-9 officer, thinking he understood exactly how the dog was feeling.

"We'll be back to get them soon," Julianne reassured Thunder, patting him on the head as they returned to Brody's SUV.

The ride out to the motel didn't take long. Zeke was pacing the length of the hallway outside the motel room door, looking agitated.

"What's wrong?" Julianne asked.

"The blood we found at the house in the woods definitely belongs to Jake, as does the blood found at the second cabin near the river."

Brody couldn't say he was surprised, after all they'd found Jake's watch there, too. And Thunder had already proven that the missing FBI agent had been there.

"I'm sorry," Julianne murmured, placing a reassuring hand on Zeke's arm. "Have faith, Zeke, there's no reason to suspect the worst. I'm sure Jake is still alive. He's worth more to the Duprees alive than dead."

Zeke abruptly shrugged her off and turned away, his fingers clenched into fists. Brody didn't know the guy, other than from the short time they'd worked together, but he had the impression that it wouldn't take much for Zeke Morrow to lose his cool.

"There you are," Max said, appearing in the doorway. "Did Zeke fill you in?"

"Yes," Julianne agreed. "We have confirmation the blood samples belong to Jake, but what about the other evidence we collected?"

Max's expression turned grim. "We found trace evidence that matches other samples in the lab. Samples that we believe belong to Angus Dupree."

Julianne's eyes widened. "Angus was actually here in Clover? Not just his henchmen?"

"That's what we believe," Max agreed. "We're heading back to headquarters, ASAP."

Brody's heart sank, even though this was nothing more than what he'd known was coming.

"Max, I'd like to stay here for a couple of days," Julianne said. "To assist in tying up the loose ends of the Otwell case."

Max's gaze darkened with suspicion. "What loose ends?"

Brody took a step closer to Julianne, wordlessly offering his support.

"For one thing, we don't know who the driver of the getaway car was," she said. "And for another, we need to interrogate former Deputy Rick Meyer to understand what role he played in all of this."

"We?" Max echoed, his brow furrowed in a deep frown. "What are you really trying to tell me, Agent Martinez?"

Brody almost winced at the stricken expression in Julianne's eyes.

"Once we're finished with the Dupree case, I'm considering returning here to Clover, Texas. I need some time with Brody." The words came out in a rush and Brody reached over to take her hand in his.

"Really?" Max crossed his arms over his chest. "And here I was thinking of offering Sheriff Kenner a job."

Julianne's eyes widened. "You were?"

"You were?" Brody echoed in shocked surprise.

Max nodded. "You were accepted into the program years ago, no reason to believe you won't be accepted again. We could use someone with your skills, although it's going to take some time for you to get through the FBI academy."

The thought of attending the FBI academy was overwhelming. He'd be starting from the bottom, but when he glanced over at Julianne and saw the shimmering hope reflected in her dark eyes, he knew he couldn't let her down.

Not again.

"I'd be honored to join the team," he said, reaching out to shake Max's hand. "But I need to finish up the case I've built against Otwell first. I hope you understand."

"Of course," Max said with a nod. The SAC glanced at his watch. "Julianne, as much as I'd like to give you a few days off, I need you to come with us. We're hitting the road soon."

Julianne looked devastated, but Brody drew her close

and wrapped his arm around her shoulders. "It's okay, Max needs you more than I do."

She turned and hugged him, squeezing tightly as if she'd never let him go. He buried his nose in her luxurious dark hair, inhaling the familiar sweet scent of honeysuckle.

"I was hoping to stay," she whispered.

"Me, too." He closed his eyes for a long moment. "But I promise I'll see you soon."

She pulled back far enough to gaze up at him. "I'm holding you to that promise, Brody."

He gave her another quick kiss, wishing they had more time. "I hope you do," he agreed. "Because I'm not going to make the same mistake I did six years ago."

She smiled then, a tremulous smile. "And you'll pick up Cooper and Hawk?"

"Of course. I'll bring them with me." He tucked a strand of her long silky hair behind her ear. "Just give me a couple of days, okay?"

"Okay." She kissed him, then eased out of his arms. "Ready when you are," she told Max.

Her boss was watching them with a speculative gleam in his eye, but he didn't say anything. "Let's get ready to roll."

Brody turned and walked back to his vehicle. Leaving Julianne wasn't easy, but knowing he'd see her again, soon, gave him the strength to do what needed to be done.

Putting the final nails in the case he'd built against Nathan Otwell and his former deputy, Rick Meyer.

Julianne was exhausted by the time they arrived back in Billings, Montana. After Max had provided an update to the rest of the team, Dylan O'Leary pulled her aside. Since she was standing up for his fiancée, Zara, as one of her bridesmaids, she assumed that he wanted to talk about the wedding plans. Instead he asked for a favor.

"Do you have time to run an errand with me?" he asked.

Shoving her travel-weary exhaustion aside, she smiled and nodded. "Absolutely. What do you need?"

"I need to pick up our rings for the wedding," he confided. "The jeweler just called to tell me they're ready."

"Oh, that sounds like fun," Julianne agreed. She followed him outside into the much-cooler-than-Texas air. "How is Zara doing, by the way?"

Dylan didn't say anything until they were settled in the front seat of his truck. "If you want to know the truth, I'm worried about her."

"Worried?" Julianne knew Dylan's fiancée was currently in training with a group of other potential FBI agents at Quantico. "Is she having trouble with the training?"

Dylan glanced at her. "More like someone is giving them trouble. There seems to have been a few mishaps."

She didn't like the sound of that. "What do you mean?"

"Several trainees fell when the ropes on the obstacle course broke. Thankfully, there were no serious injuries. Zara told me that she and several other cadets examined the ropes and believe they were cut."

Cut ropes? Julianne had difficulty wrapping her mind around the implication. "Who would do such a thing? At Quantico, no less?"

"Exactly," Dylan agreed. "There was also some stray gunfire during a handgun training session. It's almost as if someone is out to purposefully hurt or sabotage the new trainees."

Julianne mulled that over as Dylan pulled into the parking lot of a high-class jewelry store. "It's possible some of us from our unit could help investigate. Does Max know about this?"

Dylan shook his head as he slid out from behind the wheel. "No, I haven't told Max and I'd appreciate it if you'd keep this conversation confidential. Zara and her team want to take the lead on investigating this on their own. After all, they'll soon be FBI agents in their own right."

She grimaced, not liking the thought of Zara and the other trainees being in possible danger, yet at the same time, Max didn't really have jurisdiction to butt in, either. Their motto was to find and eliminate domestic terrorism and in this case, that meant bringing down the Dupree crime family once and for all.

"I won't say anything yet," she assured him. "But if anything else happens, you really need to confide in Max. Before things escalate to the point someone is seriously injured."

"I can go along with that plan," he agreed.

Dylan held the door open for her, so she led the way inside. Several long glass cases spanned the room, filled with expensive jewelry, the lights from above causing the stones to sparkle brightly.

She peered at the glitter of emeralds, rubies and diamonds as Dylan spoke with the manager. When the woman pulled out the wedding rings, Julianne peered over to get a better look. Zara's diamond was beautiful and she couldn't help wondering what it would be like to have an engagement ring of her own from Brody.

Whoa, wait a minute. Sure, Brody had agreed to train as an FBI agent, and she knew that meant he wanted to continue seeing her.

But marriage? Wasn't that jumping the gun just a little? After all, he hadn't even told her he loved her.

The way she loved him.

The silent words struck her hard. She loved Brody. The man he'd grown into, confident yet able to admit when he'd been wrong. The protector who instinctively wanted to shield her from harm but treated her as his equal.

Would they really get the second chance they both deserved?

* * *

"Sheriff? Attorney Jeremy Strand is here to see his client."

Brody shot out from behind his desk and strode over to where Strand waited next to the dispatcher's desk. The guy was an hour late, and it was Sunday, so there weren't any deputies around. He still had two men stationed outside Rick Meyer's hospital room. The former deputy had gotten an infection requiring him to stay longer. Brody had purposefully reduced the rest of the staff to a skeleton crew to make up for the hundreds of extra hours they'd worked gathering evidence and maintaining roadblocks during the jailbreak.

"Mr. Strand," he drawled, raking his gaze over the man dressed in a suit that cost more than Brody's car. "Kindly set your briefcase aside so I can verify you're not carrying a weapon."

The attorney scowled and set his briefcase on top of the dispatcher's desk. Brody was about to tell him to remove it, when the attorney whipped out a gun.

"Stand back, Sheriff," the attorney said. "And you," he turned to Sandra, the dispatcher on duty, "Put your hands in the air where I can see them."

Brody drilled the attorney with an intense gaze. "You're making a big mistake, counselor," he warned, angry that he'd been caught off guard. "Put the gun away, nice and easy."

"No! I want you to walk over to open that jail cell, right now!"

For a moment Julianne's image flashed into his mind, but he refused to be distracted by the possibility of never seeing her again. No way was he letting Otwell out of jail, not after everything he'd gone through to put him in there, not just once but twice.

"Okay, hold onto your britches. Let's just stay calm so

no one gets hurt." Brody was trying to stall for time, but he wasn't sure doing so would help. It wasn't as if he was expecting anyone to arrive anytime soon.

He didn't dare glance at Sandra, afraid to see the fear and horror in the dispatcher's eyes.

Abruptly the door to the building burst open and Brody didn't hesitate. He rushed the attorney, grabbing the wrist holding the gun and twisting the weapon out of his grasp. Then he wrenched the guy's arm behind his back and quickly slapped the silver bracelets on, restraining him.

"Good timing, Hanson," he said to his senior deputy.

"Thank Sandra, she's the one who left the microphone open on the dispatch speaker so I could hear what was going down. Good thing I wasn't far."

Brody shoved Jeremy Strand into the cell adjacent to Otwell's. After reading the attorney his rights, he glanced between the two men. "Looks like you'll need a new attorney, Nate. And Strand, if I were you, I wouldn't try to defend yourself in this case. Not when you have three witnesses who heard you attempt to break Nate out of jail for the second time."

Strand glared at him, but exercised his right to remain silent for which Brody was grateful. They'd need to obtain a search warrant on Strand's vehicle in an attempt to find evidence of either Otwell or Royce being inside recently. If they were, there's a good chance Strand had assisted with the jailbreak. If not, there was still the fact that the lawyer had tried to break him out of jail today.

Either way, he believed this was the last piece of the puzzle. Otwell, Meyer and Strand would all end up in jail for the rest of their lives.

Over the next few days, between caring for the two puppies, Cooper and Hawk, Brody and his next in command, Dan Hanson, tied up the remaining loose ends of their case.

Hanson's attitude had changed dramatically for the better, for which Brody was sincerely grateful. They were able to match up key evidence from all the various crime scenes, connecting everything together in an iron-clad case.

Not one of the arrested men would be freed from jail for a long, long time.

When they finished, he looked at Hanson. "How would you like to be the interim sheriff?"

"What?" Hanson looked dumbfounded. "Where are you going?"

"Billings, Montana." Brody broke into a wide grin. "I've already given my notice to the mayor. He'll be glad to know you'll be stepping in to help take charge in my absence."

Hanson looked surprised, then nodded. "I appreciate your faith in me, Sheriff."

"Just make sure you keep your attitude to yourself," Brody warned him. "Don't let this position go to your head."

Hanson actually looked embarrassed. "I've learned my lesson, Sheriff. Watching Agent Martinez and her K-9 officer in action was humbling."

"Good."

After making sure the DA was looped into the evidence they'd found on the case, Brody made arrangements to fly to Billings. He knew he'd have to return at some point to testify, but for now, his plan was to take Cooper and Hawk with him to meet up with Julianne. Almost two weeks had passed, and he was anxious to see her. The days they'd spent apart had been more difficult than he'd imagined.

He walked into the headquarters for the FBI Tactical K-9 unit, the two puppies leaping around on their leashes, and immediately ran into Julianne.

"Brody! You're here!"

His heart stuttered when she rushed over and threw her arms around his neck. He clutched her close, breathing in her honeysuckle scent as he lifted her off the floor and spun her in a circle before setting her back on her feet.

"I've missed you so much," he said, before capturing her mouth in a tender kiss.

"I've missed you, too." She smiled up at him. "It's so good to see you, Brody. Oh, and you brought Cooper and Hawk!"

She bent down to cuddle the pups before rising once again to her feet.

He stared into her wide, brown eyes, trying to remember the speech he'd rehearsed on the flight over, but the practiced words escaped him. "I arrested Otwell's lawyer. He was the guy who helped him escape from the prison van," he blurted.

"Really? So his lawyer, Royce and Deputy Meyer were helping him. No wonder he was able to escape."

"Yeah, but we've got them in custody. They'll never be able to hurt anyone ever again."

"So it's finally over?"

"Yeah." He continued to hold her close, unable to find the will to let her go, the pups winding around their feet. "And you were right, the woman's body we found did belong to Lilly Ramos." His voice broke for a moment, and he was thankful the old guilt seemed to be gone for good. "She'll be given the proper burial she deserves."

"I'm so sorry, Brody. I'm sure that was very difficult for you." Her eyes were troubled as they searched his.

This was the moment of truth. "I've spent the last week attending church services and making inroads toward rebuilding my faith." He swallowed hard. "I've learned that God forgave me a long time ago, and the only person I needed to forgive for messing up all those years ago is me. With God's help, I've been able to let go of the guilt of my past mistakes."

"Oh, Brody." Julianne's dark eyes shimmered with tears. "I'm so glad to hear that you've renewed your relationship with God."

"Me, too." He kissed her again, wishing he could whisk her away someplace where they could be alone. But each time he tried for perfect timing, it never happened, so he decided there was no reason to wait a moment longer. "Julianne, I want you to know how much I love you. There's never been another woman for me, not since you. I always loved you."

She swiped at her eyes, her smile hesitant. "Are you sure? Six years ago you didn't love me enough to believe me over Nate."

Shame washed over him. "I was wrong, but it wasn't because I didn't love you. I was determined to be loyal to Nate. He was the one who stood up for me at the juvenile center. And if we're being honest here, I didn't appreciate your refusal to support me, either."

She let out a sigh. "I guess I can understand that. We were both young and immature, not certain of our love."

"But not anymore," he said firmly. "The past is in the past. I don't want to scare you off, but I love you with all my heart. That love gave me the strength to quit my job as sheriff of Clover County. I'm ready to start the next phase of my life. With you."

She kissed him. "I'm glad to hear it, because I love you, Brody. In all the years we've been apart, there's never been another man for me. Only you."

Hearing her repeat his words back made his heart swell with love. He crushed her close, silently rejoicing in God's plan that had brought them back together. He would have kissed her again, maybe to never stop kissing her, when a shout interrupted his thoughts.

"Julianne!"

Brody glanced up at Max's voice. "What's wrong?"

"Good to see you, Kenner. And I see you brought the puppies! Bring them along. I want you and Julianne to report to the conference room, ASAP."

Julianne pulled out of his embrace and he reluctantly let her go. They unwound the leashes, each taking one of the puppies with them as they entered the conference room. He was impressed at the team assembled there. Their expressions were serious even as they indulged in pastries from a place called Petrov's Bakery.

"What happened, Max?" Julianne said as she dropped into a chair. Brody took the seat beside her.

Max's expression was somber as he swept his gaze over the room. "I've just been notified of a bomb that exploded at a home in Northern California. A family of four was killed in the blast."

The entire group went still. The room was so quiet Brody could hear his heart thumping in his chest. Each member's gaze was riveted on their boss.

"The makeup of this explosive device is identical to one used previously by the Dupree crime family," Max continued. "At this time, we haven't found a connection between the dead family and the mobsters, but you can be sure that if we do find the Duprees are involved, we'll be heading over to investigate."

Brody didn't like the thought of Julianne being sent so far away, but of course, he wasn't about to protest, either. This was her job, and hopefully someday soon, his.

"When do you think we'll know?" Julianne asked.

Max shrugged. "You'll know as soon as I do. Stay close until we get confirmation one way or another."

The group remained solemn for a moment, before they began talking amongst themselves.

"This is going to be a tough case for Max if it turns out the Duprees are involved," Julianne said in a low voice to Brody.

"Why is that?"

"He lost someone close to him in a bomb explosion five years ago," she confided. "I think that's the main reason he's paired up with Opal. The boxer's specialty is to find explosive devices."

Brody remembered the uncanny connection between all the FBI agents and their respective K-9 partners. "You're right, that will be tough."

"The fact that the bomb makeup is the same as the one used by the Duprees makes me think it's highly likely they're involved," she said thoughtfully. "I hate to say this, Brody, but our reunion here appears to be short-lived. It looks like I may be heading to Northern California soon."

"I understand," he said, stroking Cooper's soft fur. "And don't worry, I have no intention of standing in your way. I've learned you can take care of yourself, Julianne, even though I'd be lying if I told you I don't want to tag along, because I'd go in a heartbeat. Not that I don't trust your team or Thunder to keep you safe, I do. But all of that aside, I'd feel much better if I was the one backing you up."

She smiled. "I know, Brody. Trust me, I feel the same way."

They took the puppies with them outside into the bright sunlight. Brody caught his breath at the magnificence of the mountains looming over the horizon. He captured her hand and tugged her close, knowing he needed to move quickly. "Julianne? Would you do me the honor of becoming my wife?"

She blinked and frowned, staring at him as if he'd lost his marbles. "What?"

He wasn't sure if her confusion was a good thing or not, and his mouth went dry. "Will you please marry me? As soon as possible? As soon as we can get a license? Before you're sent to California and I have to return to the east coast for training?"

"Here?" She still looked dazed. "You want to get married here in Montana?"

"Yes. I know it probably sounds crazy, but I don't want to lose you." He couldn't bear the thought. "Our time together over the next few months is going to be limited, and we'll likely be on opposite coasts for longer than I care to think about, so will you please, please, marry me?"

Abruptly she laughed and engulfed him in an overwhelming embrace. "Oh, Brody, yes. Yes, I'll marry you. Now, tomorrow or whenever you want."

"Thank you," he muttered, burying his face in her hair. The puppies played at their feet. "For a moment I thought you were going to turn me down."

"Never," she promised, leaning back to gaze adoringly up at him. "Now that I've found you again, I have no intention of letting you go. I want us to always be there for each other, no matter how many miles there are between us."

Brody was humbled by her impassioned speech. "I want that, too. I promise to support you throughout our careers." Then he couldn't help but grin. "You've made me the happiest man in the entire world. I love you."

"And I love you, too. Now and forever."

Brody's throat clogged with emotion and he raised his

eyes to the sky, silently thanking God for bringing Julianne back into his life.

 And this time, he'd never let her go.

* * * * *

*If you enjoyed SHERIFF by Laura Scott, look for the
other books in the CLASSIFIED K-9 UNIT miniseries:*

*GUARDIAN by Terri Reed
SPECIAL AGENT by Valerie Hansen
BOUNTY HUNTER by Lynette Eason
BODYGUARD by Shirlee McCoy
TRACKER by Lenora Worth
CLASSIFIED K-9 UNIT CHRISTMAS by Terri Reed
and Lenora Worth*

Dear Reader,

I hope you enjoyed *Sheriff*, the second book in the Classified K-9 Unit series. I'm honored to be in such great company with such amazing authors. All the books in the K-9 series are wonderful, and while each book stands alone, the ongoing suspense kept me on the edge of my seat as I read the entire series.

Reunion stories are one of my favorites to write and I hope you enjoy them, too. When K-9 FBI Agent Julianne Martinez returns to her home state of Texas, the last person she expects to come to her rescue is Sheriff Brody Kenner, her ex-boyfriend. Now that Julianne is a key witness in Brody's case, the two are forced to work together and to reconcile their past. Will they be able to heal the wounds from their breakup to find love the second time around?

I hope you enjoy Brody and Julianne's story, along with the other books in the K-9 series. I love hearing from my readers. If you're interested in contacting me or signing up for my newsletter, please visit my website at www.laurascottbooks.com. I'm also on Facebook at Laura Scott Books Author and on Twitter, @laurascottbooks.

Yours in faith,
Laura Scott

SPECIAL EXCERPT FROM

Love Inspired
SUSPENSE

An FBI agent must protect his prime suspect in a series of bombings...without falling for her.

Read on for an excerpt from Valerie Hansen's
SPECIAL AGENT,
the next book in the exciting new series,
CLASSIFIED K-9 UNIT.

Katerina Garwood was halfway between one of the stables and the house, heading for her old suite, when she saw an imposing black vehicle pass beneath the ornate wrought iron arch at the foot of the drive. Unexpected company was all she needed. If her father came outside to see who it was and caught her trespassing on his precious property he'd be furious. Well, so be it. There was no way she could run and hide in time to avoid encountering the new arrival—and perhaps her irate dad, as well.

Chin high, she paused in the wide, hard-packed drive and shaded her eyes. The SUV reminded her of one that had assisted the county sheriff on the worst day of her life. The day when all her dreams of a happy future had vanished like a puff of smoke.

Dark-tinted windows kept her from getting a good look at the driver until he stopped, opened his door and stepped partway out. Prepared to tell him to go to the house if he needed to speak to someone in charge, she took one look and was momentarily speechless. The blond, blue-eyed man was so imposing and had such a powerful presence he sent her usually normal reactions whirling. When he spoke, his deep voice magnified those unsettling feelings.

"Katerina Garwood?"

"Do I know you?"

"No, but I know you. I'm Special Agent West. I'd like to talk to you about Vern Kowalski."

"I have nothing to say." She started to turn away.

"This is not a social call, Ms. Garwood." He flashed a badge and blocked her path. "I suggest you reconsider."

"FBI? You have to be kidding. I am so normal, so boring, that until recently people hardly noticed me."

"They do now, I take it."

She blushed and rolled her eyes. "Oh, yeah."

"Then you'll understand why I need to speak with you."

Don't miss
SPECIAL AGENT by Valerie Hansen,
available wherever
Love Inspired® Suspense ebooks are sold.

www.LoveInspired.com